DOLPHIN DREAMS

ALSO BY CATHERINE HAPKA

Heart of a Dolphin

DOLPHIN DREAMS

CATHERINE HAPKA

SCHOLASTIC INC.

ISBN 978-1-338-13642-5

10 9 8 7 6 5 4 3 2 1   17 18 19 20 21

Printed in the U.S.A.   40

First printing 2017

Book design by Mary Claire Cruz

Avery

"You're planning to wear *that*?"

"Yeah. Why?" I glanced down, hoping I hadn't spilled something on my shorts or, worse, my favorite T-shirt.

My cousin Kady wrinkled her nose. "You're twelve, not two," she said. "Nobody wears big, baggy shirts with pictures of dolphins on them around here."

Her older brother, Cameron, looked up from his cereal and laughed. "So speaketh the fashion princess," he intoned. "Better change into your best ball gown, Avery. Otherwise Kady won't be seen with you."

Kady rolled her eyes in Cam's general direction. Then she grabbed me by the wrist and dragged me toward the stairs. "You can borrow one of my shirts. But hurry. My friends are probably already there."

Soon we were in her room. Our room. Well, sort of, anyway.

I glanced at the air mattress crammed into the corner by Kady's overflowing closet, wondering how my life had turned upside down so suddenly.

Never mind—I knew exactly why. It was because my father had decided he didn't want to be married anymore. That was why Mom and I had moved halfway across the country to Southern California to stay with her sister's family.

Kady was only a year older than me—fourteen and a half months, we used to say when we were little. So that had seemed like a silver lining. At least if I had to leave everyone and everything I'd ever known behind, I would have a built-in best friend in California.

Only it hadn't worked out that way at all.

"Here, try this." Kady tossed a wrinkled blouse at me. "It should fit okay."

The blouse was yellow with sparkles on the collar. When we were little, Kady would have made fun of a shirt like that. She used to be a tomboy, like me, who loved stuff like catching tadpoles in the creek and camping out in the backyard. And dolphin tees.

I touched the soft fabric of my shirt. So far, the only good thing about moving here was seeing real live dolphins in the Pacific. Cam had taken me to the beach last week, only a day or two after we'd arrived, as soon as he found out I liked them. We'd stayed there, perched on big, smooth rocks, until we finally spotted a pod playing out past the breakers.

It had been amazing. I'd held my breath as I watched them leap and spin, their wet gray skin shining under the bright California sun. Dolphins have been my favorite animal for as long as I can remember, but the only place I'd ever seen one before that was in a big tank at the aquarium back home.

So I guess that was the real silver lining. Not Kady, but the dolphins, which Cam had assured me swam near that beach all the time. He knew, since it was his favorite surfing spot. All I had to do was walk the eight blocks to get there and I could watch them for hours if I wanted. For a second I thought about doing that right then instead of going to the mall with Kady and her friends.

But it was the first time Kady had invited me to do anything, and I was still hoping she'd turn back into my fun, friendly cousin from years ago. So I decided to go. Still, that didn't mean I had to do everything she said. "Thanks, but I think I'll keep this on," I told her, tugging down the hem of my T-shirt.

"You can't." She crossed her arms. "Seriously. It's like a major fashion faux pas."

I didn't know what that meant, and I didn't care. "Come on, let's go if we're going." I dropped the yellow blouse on her bed and headed for the door.

She muttered something I couldn't quite hear and followed. "Don't blame me if my friends make fun of you," she said as she pushed past me to lead the way downstairs.

Her friends didn't make fun of me. Mostly because they totally ignored me. We met them at the mall, which looked pretty much like every other mall I'd ever been to back home. It wasn't like the fancy outdoor palm tree–lined shopping centers down in LA that I'd seen on TV and in the movies. When I said that, Kady and the others all looked at me as if I had two heads and three noses.

So I kept pretty quiet after that, which wasn't like me. Normally I can talk about anything with anyone. I just couldn't think of anything to say to these girls who only seemed interested in boys and clothes and lip gloss and celebrity gossip. Weren't there any normal kids in California?

"Let's go in here," one of the girls said, stopping in front of a bookstore.

Kady wrinkled her nose. "Ew, why? School's out for summer, remember?"

"Whoo!" another girl cheered.

The first girl hurried toward the magazine rack near the front. "Duh. New *Cosmo*."

As they gathered around some dumb fashion magazine, I noticed a girl around my age watching out of the corner of her eye. She was standing by a bookshelf nearby, paging through a large hardcover book with a bright blue cover.

She caught me looking and turned away quickly, her cheeks going pink. She was shorter than me, with light-brown skin and thick dark hair that looked like it wanted to escape from the braid down her back.

When she turned, I got a better look at the book she was holding. It had a cute photo of a leaping dolphin on the cover. "Hey," I blurted out, stepping closer. "I have that book—my dad got it for me for Christmas." I gulped, pushing thoughts of my father back out of reach. "It's really good. Do you like dolphins, too?"

The girl blinked at me. Her eyes were big and dark, with long lashes. "Um, yeah," she said, her gaze darting back and forth from me to Kady and back again.

Just then Kady turned around. "Hey, Avery," she called, marching toward me. "Is that girl bothering you?"

"What? No." I glanced at the girl. "We were just talking."

Kady grabbed my arm. "Let's go." She shot the other girl a nasty look. "*Pardon* us."

Before I knew it, we were back out in the mall aisle. "What was that all about?" I said, shaking my arm loose from her iron grip. "I was just—"

"You shouldn't talk to people like that." Kady cut me off with a frown.

"People like what?" I asked.

Just then her friends rushed over. "Ew, was that Maria Flores?" one of them exclaimed.

"Yes." Kady stared at me. "Don't blame Avery, though. She doesn't know what Maria's like."

"So what's she like?" I said, perplexed and a little annoyed by how they were acting. "She seemed nice enough to me."

One of the other girls widened her eyes dramatically. "Oh wow, Avery, she's bad news. She lives in this totally nasty neighborhood, and I heard her older brother's in a gang!"

"Really?" Now I was surprised. There weren't any gangs back home. I glanced back at Maria, wondering if what Kady and her friends were saying could possibly be true.

"Yeah, her sister's bad news, too." Kady shook her head at me. "They should definitely be avoided. Now come on, let's get a soda or something. I need to wash the bad taste out of my mouth."

2

Maria

The girl in the dolphin shirt glanced back once while Kady Swanson dragged her away like a cougar dragging its prey, but I pretended I didn't see. Who was she? Related to Kady, maybe? It seemed a likely guess, since I could see the family resemblance between the two of them—same bright blue eyes, raw-sienna hair, sharp little chin, and pale freckly cheeks. The only thing the new girl was missing was the haughty expression, which Kady used like a weapon at school, striking at those of us she deemed less than worthy. I closed my eyes and smiled, imagining drawing a cartoon of that, with daggers flying out of Kady's icy blue eyes . . .

"Maria?" a familiar voice called.

I opened my eyes and spun around, nearly dropping the book on my toes. Josie was striding toward me. Not walking, not ambling, but moving with purpose and energy, like the athlete she was. Josie never did anything without purpose. Or without the big smile she was beaming at me right now.

"I've been looking everywhere for you, *chica*," she said, tossing her sleek brown ponytail over her shoulder. How did her hair always stay so smooth and perfect, when mine exploded into a rat's nest the second it dried? We had the same mother, the same father. It didn't seem fair.

"I was just browsing." I tucked the dolphin book back on the shelf before she could see it and start asking questions. The last thing I wanted was to become the topic of conversation at family dinner that night, pinned in my chair like the moths and weevils in Nico's old childhood insect collection. If things worked out the way I hoped, well, the family would find out about it soon enough. If not, I figured they never needed to know.

I followed Josie out of the bookstore, glad to see that Kady Swanson and her cronies had disappeared. I was still a little bit curious about the dolphin girl, but not curious enough to risk the wrath of Kady. Even though the dolphin girl had seemed nice, she was with someone not-so-nice, which made me think she might be not-so-nice herself. As my *abuelita* liked to say, *"Dios los cría y ellos se juntan"*—birds of a feather flock together.

"Hey." Josie poked me out of my thoughts. "Are you daydreaming again, little sister? Wake up—there's a sale at the department store. Maybe we can find you a new swimsuit."

"I already have a swimsuit." I was tired of shopping. The air conditioning was too cold, making goose pimples dance up and down my arms and legs. The only reason I'd come at all was for a peek at those dolphin books.

"That ratty old blue thing?" Josie snorted.

"Don't worry, Mom gave me money to get you a new one."

I wasn't sure why it mattered. Hardly anybody saw me in that suit. I avoided the busy public beaches, preferring my own company to the chaos of crowds. As my sister charged off toward the department store, I trailed along after her, dreaming about going to my favorite hidden cove.

* * *

Hours later, I finally picked my way down the steep, rocky trail leading into Spotted Dolphin Cove. That wasn't its real name—the place was so obscure it wasn't labeled on any map I'd ever seen. But I'd named it when I'd first discovered it two summers earlier. Since my friends Iggy and Carmen had moved back to Mexico with their family last year, I'd only ever run into someone else at the cove a few times. Most people didn't know it was there. The entrance wasn't easy to find and the trail looked like it led to nowhere. And even the ones who found it usually didn't like it—the beach was rocky and narrow, and there was no cell phone reception, and the water was too calm for anything but beginner surfing. But I didn't mind. I liked it for other reasons.

I dropped my surfboard and the backpack with my sketchpad and other stuff in it onto the rocky sand and stepped to the water's edge, letting the surf roll in and cool my toes. Squinting against the bright bursts of sunlight reflecting off the constantly moving water, I scanned the cove for signs of life. A gull was circling lazily overhead, letting out the occasional raw squawk. But that wasn't what I was looking for.

A smile spread over my face as I finally spotted a dorsal fin breaking the water. A second later the dolphin leaped up, arcing toward me, followed by another and another. I grabbed my board and waded in, not bothering with the leash. My parents didn't know I swam in the cove by myself, but then again, they'd never really asked. When I reached the drop-off where the water got deep, I belly flopped onto the board, paddling out to the middle of the cove with my arms.

The dolphins were close now—only the length of three or four surfboards away. I sat up on my board, dangling one leg off either side while I watched them play. How many were there today? It was hard to keep track of the sleek gray bodies as they popped into view one after another. I recognized the one with the crooked snout, and the smaller, leaner one that I called Little Sister. The rest were just a blur of dove-gray grace.

Then I saw another familiar shape burst into view. "Seurat!" I blurted out.

This was the dolphin I'd seen the very first time I'd come here—the funny-looking one with white dots mottling his smooth dark skin. That first day I hadn't known why he looked so different from the others, but he'd reminded me of something a pointillist painter might have created. That was why I'd named him Seurat, after Georges-Pierre Seurat. The human Seurat was a famous French painter who pretty much invented pointillism, which is just creating images out of lots and lots of dots. If he'd ever painted a dolphin, it would have looked like my Seurat.

Later, I'd looked up dolphins online, trying to figure out if there was something wrong with my pointillist dolphin. But it turned out he was a whole different species from the regular bottlenoses he hung out with. As best I could figure, he was a pantropical spotted dolphin, a species that loved warm tropical water and so usually didn't come this far up the California coast, just north enough to make the water a little chilly once you left the sun-warmed surf line. But it seemed Seurat liked it here, because I'd seen him lots of times since.

I laughed as Seurat threw himself all the way out of the water, splashing down in a spray of foam and droplets that mixed with the white spots dotted all over him. He was always playful, even by dolphin standards.

"Show-off!" I called, wiggling my toes to stop my board from drifting sideways with the current.

I waited for Seurat to leap again, but after that

one big effort he seemed content to float around and watch the others.

I did that, too, paddling with my hands and feet now and then to keep myself from drifting too far out from the beach. Not because I was afraid—I'd been swimming in the ocean since we'd moved here when I was four years old, and I felt as comfortable on my surfboard (or even just swimming) as I did on dry land. More comfortable, actually. Out here, I didn't have to worry about saying something stupid that would make mean kids like Kady Swanson laugh at me. Out here, there was nobody judging me or thinking I was weird because I didn't talk much and always had my head bent over my sketchpad. Out here, I didn't always remember to miss Iggy and Carmen, who'd left me adrift like a ship with no sails or engine when they moved away.

So being out on the water wasn't the problem, deep or shallow, but I still made sure to keep myself back from the dolphins. The dolphins were my friends, and I was pretty sure they liked having me around, but they got nervous if I came *too* close. I could respect that. I didn't like people crowding in around me, either.

After a while I noticed the sun was sinking lower out over the sea and realized it would be dinnertime soon. It was my turn to set the table, so I'd better not be late unless I wanted to hear about it from my mother. Reluctantly, I started paddling back toward shore.

"Bye, dolphins," I called to my friends. Most of them didn't pay any attention to me, but Seurat swam along behind me halfway to the beach, his funny spotted face popping up to watch me stand and catch a small wave back to shore.

When I got there, my sketchpad was falling half out of the bag where I'd dropped it, and I imagined it sending up disappointed feelings at me. I grabbed it and stuffed it back into the depths of the bag, telling myself it didn't matter if I hadn't done any work on my sketch today. There was still plenty of time, and I didn't want to rush it. No, it had to be perfect, and that took as long as it took.

In any case, it had been worth missing an afternoon's work to spend time with my dolphin friends. I whistled once in farewell, then grabbed board and bag and started the climb up the narrow, steep, twisting path out of the cove and toward home.

3

Avery

I was having my favorite dream again. I'd had some version of it for as long as I could remember. This time I was swimming deep down in a gorgeous blue ocean, breathing without thinking and swimming without effort. All around me were dolphins—big ones, little ones, bold ones, shy ones, all of them gray and beautiful and full of fun. We played tag and did flips, and it was the best thing ever . . .

Then a sudden clatter yanked me out of the dream.

I sat up and rubbed my eyes, groggy and annoyed. What had awakened me? It wasn't Kady—she was sound asleep, snoring softly, her glossy reddish-brown hair spread out over her pillowcase—real silk, she'd been sure to tell me proudly, as if I cared.

Then the clatter came again, along with a mumbled curse from the hallway just outside the bedroom. Squinting against the bright morning sunlight, I climbed out of bed and stepped over to ease open the door. I definitely didn't want to wake up Kady. I'd only been sharing a room with her for a little over a week, but I already knew she wasn't a morning person.

Cam was in the narrow upstairs hallway with a surfboard under each arm. It looked like he was trying to wrestle them down the stairs, and they were winning. The house had a funny staircase with curved iron railings and two landings, so Cam had to stick the boards out over the rail to fit them down.

He glanced up at me with a sheepish smile.

"Avery! Hi," he said quietly. "I was afraid you were Kady."

I smiled and stepped forward to help, grabbing one end of the longer, blue-patterned surfboard and helping him maneuver it. When we got both boards downstairs, he leaned them up against the wall by the front door. He was dressed in a T-shirt and striped board shorts that came almost all the way down to his knobby knees.

"Sorry if I woke you up," he said. "I took my boards up to my room to wax them last night."

"That's okay." I didn't tell him about the dream, of course. Nobody knew about that. Not even Mom.

Cam stuck his feet into a pair of battered flip-flops on the shoe mat by the door. "Want to come surfing with me?" he said. "Supposed to be some clean waves this morning."

"Oh." I wondered if he'd forgotten about The Incident. It had happened a pretty long time ago, after all. Even if it seemed like yesterday to me sometimes. "Um, no thanks."

"You can use my extra board." He gestured toward the two surfboards. "Or maybe you can borrow Kady's. She never uses it, anyway."

"I don't know . . ."

"Come on." Cam had a nice smile—sort of like Mom's and Aunt Janice's, but with one crooked tooth on the bottom that made him look mischievous and unique. "Lots of dolphins out this time of morning."

I hesitated, flashing back to my dream. I'd walked out to the beach the day before, but it had been hard to see much with all the bright sunlight flashing on the swells. Once I'd thought I saw a couple of dolphins far out, but it might have just been more waves.

"You're a California girl now," Cam added. "That means you have to learn to surf. It's the law."

"Really?" I blurted out before I caught myself—and the sly little grin on my cousin's face. "Ha-ha, very funny!"

He grinned. "Come on, give it a try. What have you got to lose?"

Easy for him to say. I was pretty sure by now that he'd forgotten all about what had happened the last time my family had come to visit his. It was five summers ago, and I'd been obsessed with collecting shells on the beach. I'd spent most of my time wandering along staring at the sand in search of more treasures. Then one day I'd followed a pretty little limpet shell that was being pulled away by the receding waters—and I hadn't seen a big wave coming in. It had knocked me down and tumbled me around, dragging me back out to sea. Time had seemed to stop as I'd scrabbled at the wet sand, unable to see or breathe or scream, not sure which way was up. There was scratchy sand in my swimsuit and under my fingernails and in my eyes and nose and mouth, choking and blinding me. It was horrible! I'd been sure I was drowning. It seemed like forever before Uncle Phil saw me and hurried to scoop me out of the water and carry me back to dry land.

I'd spent the rest of that trip far away from the beach. On our last day, my dad had tried to talk me into going back in the water so I wouldn't get a phobia, bribing me with a triple-scoop ice-cream cone. But as soon as I'd set foot on the sand, my heart had started pounding and my arms and legs had started shaking and I'd felt like I was drowning all over again. I'd run screaming back up the steps leading up to the street, dropping my ice cream on the way. Ever since, I'd been terrified to swim anywhere except in a pool.

Things were so much easier in my dreams, when I swam around as easily as the dolphins all around me. So maybe that was a sign, especially now that I was living here with real dolphins so close. Maybe enough time had passed. Maybe if I got over my fear I'd actually be able to turn my dream into reality someday . . .

I guess I took too long to respond, because Cam turned away and grabbed the smaller board, the red one. As he reached for the door, I stepped forward.

"I guess I might come along just to watch," I said. "Can you wait while I get dressed?"

He glanced at me, his expression surprised and pleased. "Cool, sure."

I raced upstairs and then tiptoed into the bedroom to grab my bathing suit and a pair of shorts to go over it. Kady moaned and turned over, so I tiptoed back out and got dressed in the bathroom.

When I got back downstairs, Cam was waiting with two travel mugs—the kind my dad used on his daily commute. But I wasn't going to think about my dad . . .

"Avocado-berry smoothie," Cam said, handing me one of the mugs. "To go. Let's hit it—we're burning daylight."

I took a sip of the smoothie, which was thick and cold and sweet. "Right behind you," I said.

Cam headed over and picked up the red board again. "Why don't you grab the longboard, just in case you decide to give it a try?"

"Sure." I was pretty sure I wasn't going more than ankle deep in the ocean. But I picked up the blue surfboard, which was lighter than it looked. Why not? Bringing it didn't mean I had to use it.

And I didn't—not that day, anyway. I just sat on the beach and watched.

Cam's surfing friends were nice. They ranged in age from a little older than me to leaving-for-college, boys and girls both. Watching them swoop and swirl along with the waves was amazing—like dolphins flipping and spinning through the air and water. I wanted to do that, but I was scared, too.

After a while Cam came in and flopped on the sand beside me, breathing hard and looking happy. "What do you think?" he asked.

"It's amazing!" I turned to watch a pretty, dark-haired girl catch a big wave. "I've never seen people surfing up close like this. It looks hard and easy at the same time." I shot him a sheepish grin. "I guess that doesn't make much sense."

"No, it totally does." He sat up and ran his hand through his hair, leaving some sand in it but not seeming to care. "That's what makes it so cool. So do you want to give it a try? I can show you some basics."

I hesitated, watching as the dark-haired girl

finished, jumping gracefully off her board as it reached the beach. She let out a whoop of joy as one of her friends jogged over to high-five her. Could I really learn to do that?

Just then a skinny kid with a shaved head got knocked off his board by a stray wave. He popped up almost immediately, laughing, but I shuddered as I flashed back to that day five years ago, the feeling of being trapped by the angry ocean.

"Not today," I told Cam. "Maybe tomorrow?"

He shrugged, looking a little disappointed. "Whatever you say. I'm heading back out."

For the rest of the morning, I couldn't stop watching Cam and the others—and wondering if this was my chance to get over my fear. If I ever wanted to work with dolphins someday, I'd have to be able to swim in the ocean, right? Besides, surfing really did look like a blast . . .

That night I had the dolphin dream again, better than ever. And when Cam knocked softly on the door in the morning, I was already in my suit with my teeth brushed, waiting.

Maria

FULL NAME: Maria Gabriela Flores

AGE: 12

ADDRESS: 27 West Manz—

"Maria!" Josie burst into our room, as loud and jarring as a thunderclap on a still day. "There you are."

I stopped typing and slammed my laptop shut before she could catch even a glimpse of what I was doing. "Don't you ever knock?" I blurted out.

She laughed. "It's my room, too, *chica*," she said. "What are you doing that's so private, huh?"

"Nothing." I flicked my eyes toward my computer, knowing the truth was lurking there in bright pixels just beneath the cover. "Um, I mean, I was just checking my e-mail to see if Igs and Car wrote."

"Oh." That got me a sympathetic look. It almost wasn't worth it, because it only reminded me that I didn't have friends anymore. Not real ones, anyway. Sure, I'd found someone else to sit with for lunch at school, a trio of kind, studious Anglo girls who were nice to everyone and seemed to sort of like me, at least a little. One of them had even invited me to her birthday party that past spring.

But school had been out for a couple of weeks now, and those girls—and everyone else at school—seemed to have forgotten all about me. At least, none of them had called or e-mailed (not that I'd gotten in touch with them, either), and, of course, none of them lived anywhere near my neighborhood. I was sure that my social sister had noticed I was lonely without my best friends living right across the street anymore.

She couldn't have any idea what that was like. Not Josefina Flores, everyone's best friend, with her athletic accomplishments and good grades and Most Likely to Succeeds. My sister, my opposite.

Josie swooped across the room and grabbed a pair of sandals off the cluttered closet floor. "Listen, you should come to the beach with me today," she said. "There were tons of kids your age there yesterday."

"No thanks. I have stuff to do." I carefully didn't look at my computer, not wanting Josie to ask about that again.

"Like what?" She stepped over to the tall bureau we shared and slipped her favorite necklace over her head. "I hope you're not hanging out at that cove of yours all the time with your nose stuck in your sketchbook. You know Mom and Papa don't like you swimming where there's no life-guard on duty."

"I swim better than most of the lifeguards do, and you know it."

She rolled her eyes but let it drop, knowing that

I could spill a few of her secrets to our parents if she spilled this one of mine. "Seriously, Maria. Iggy and Carmen weren't the only nice girls in all of California, you know. I bet you could make some new friends at the beach."

"Everyone at the beach already has friends."

She glanced at me in the bureau's age-crackled mirror, trapping me with her happy brown eyes. "Everyone wants more friends," she said with the confidence of someone who already had plenty. "Anyway, you could just go and have fun, maybe play some volleyball, show off your surfing moves . . ."

At that moment came the distinctive creak of the bathroom door opening. Papa had been promising to grease the hinges for ages, but there it was, still screaming in alarm whenever anyone opened it. I didn't really mind. With only one bathroom for five people, it was helpful to know when the place was available.

At the sound, Josie spun around, leaping toward the door. "I'm next!" she shouted, charging out into the hall as our brother, Nico, walked past wrapped in a towel.

The bathroom door creaked shut behind her, and I decided it was time to make my escape. I grabbed my sketchpad, stuffing it into my bag as I hurried out of the room and down the narrow hall to the back door. Just outside was my surfboard, and I grabbed that, too.

The neighborhood was quiet under the glare of the early-summer sun. All the churchgoers were off at St. Cecilia's like my mother, and most everyone else was sleeping in like my father. But old Señora Lozano was out front watering her flowers, so I paused to say hello. She'd lived in California for at least thirty years, according to everyone, but still didn't have much English, so it gave me a chance to practice my Spanish.

After I'd asked after her grandchildren and her cat, I moved on. I turned the corner onto Fourth Street just in time to see Manny Aguilar and a couple of his friends kicking a soccer ball along the street, shouting and laughing and insulting one another in two languages. I ducked out of sight behind a shrub until they passed, not wanting them to see me. I'd played with Manny when we were little, but in the last couple of years he'd changed. Now he and his friends were rough and loud and always wanting to insult people or break things. Carmen, a year older and wiser than Iggy and me, had told us that that happened to all boys. I knew that wasn't entirely true, since Nico had been the same forever, but I still stayed away from Manny and the others.

Most of the cove was still shaded at that time of day, and I shivered as the water washed over my feet. The waves were small and mushy, not even useful to bodysurf let alone surf for real. No dorsal fins or happy, smiling dolphin faces broke the glassy water farther out, either. I was alone except for the birds and scuttling sea creatures.

That was just as well. There would be nothing to distract me from my sketchpad.

I pulled it out of my bag and sat down cross-legged on the cool sand, wiggling around until

I found a position with no sharp stones or shells poking me in the rear end. Then I flipped the pad open, paging through drawings in all stages of work, from barely started to almost finished. I lingered over a sketch of tree branches dancing in a windstorm, wondering if I should focus on that one instead. Would it seem more artistic to the judges, more serious and worthy of their attention? But when I reached the last page and stared at my almost-finished drawing of Seurat, I knew I was right to choose that one instead.

The drawing showed the spotted dolphin leaping joyfully through the air, salty spray flying around him and gulls wheeling overhead. I was pretty sure it was the best thing I'd ever done, which was why I was planning to use it to apply to an after-school art program held at the local community college that fall. The program was open to kids from all over the county, but you had to submit a piece of your work, and, according to the Internet, less than thirty percent of applicants got accepted. It was prestigious and challenging and intensive and fantastic, and most of the kids who completed the program ended up getting accepted to really good art schools after high school, which is exactly what I wanted. Several kids from my district applied every year, but only a handful had ever been accepted.

It was a long shot for me to get in, especially since I was on the young end of the range and had never applied before—or even ever taken a real art class outside of the ones at school. But I had to try. It sounded like an incredible opportunity to learn from real working artists, people who might be able to help me figure out how to convince my family that art could be a worthwhile career, just like being a teacher or a scientist or an engineer. Because right now they acted as if my drawing was a waste of time, time that would be better spent studying or cleaning my room or otherwise being useful and practical and normal. Besides that, the other students in the program would all be art geeks like me. Who knew? In a place like that, I might even meet a few kids who got me—kids who could become real friends.

Trying not to think too much about that—why get my hopes up, after all?—I reached for a graphite pencil and bent over the page, ready to get to work.

5

Avery

At my first real surfing lesson on Saturday, Cam claimed the waves were tiny and calm. But they looked enormous to me.

"It'll be fine." Cam shot me an encouraging smile. "I'll help you through the breaking waves, and you can hang on to the board the whole time. That'll help, right? You can just chill and get used to being out there for a while, no pressure."

I forced myself to nod. I'd finally reminded him about The Incident, so he'd promised not to push me too hard. But he said if I never actually made it into the water, he wasn't going to be able to teach me much. He was joking, I think, but I knew he was right. So I'd agreed to try floating around on his spare surfboard out past the big waves.

Getting through the breakers was terrifying. A few times I almost turned and ran back to shore. I just kept remembering that helpless feeling of being grabbed and twisted by the ocean, dragged underwater and unable to breathe . . .

But Cam was ahead of me, pulling my surfboard, and he didn't slow down. So I just held my breath and gripped as tightly as I could, trying not to think about anything until we made it through the breakers.

Once I was out there, it was actually kind of fun. I tried not to think about how I was in the Pacific Ocean, instead pretending I was in the community pool back home. Then I just lay on my stomach on the board and floated, watching Cam and the other surfers from a whole new angle. It was nice being out there in the sunshine, my hands and legs trailing in the cool water. Cam and his friends came to check on me whenever they were out waiting for a wave. Once I even thought I saw a dolphin leaping by on the horizon, though the sun was in my eyes and I wasn't sure. And when it was time to go home, Cam dragged me up to a small wave and helped me ride it in to shore on my stomach, like I was bodyboarding. It was fun, and I hardly thought about The Incident at all.

So by my next lesson on Sunday afternoon, I was feeling a little more confident. I agreed to let Cam teach me a little more about real surfing this time, though I didn't make any promises about trying it yet.

"No, it's like this." Cam jumped on his board, which was lying on the sand near mine. He bent his knees, showing me the stance he wanted.

I tried to imitate him, crouching down and sticking out my arms. "Better?" I asked.

"Good enough." Cam straightened up and shaded his eyes, glancing out toward the water. "Okay, let's see you pop up one more time."

I obeyed, flopping onto the board on my stomach, pretending to paddle, and then jumping to my feet. It was supposed to happen in one smooth motion, but it felt kind of awkward. Still, a few of his friends who were taking a break on the beach let out a whoop or a cheer.

I smiled over at them, taking a little bow right there on the board. "How was that?" I asked Cam.

"Good, at least for a grommet." He grinned. "Want to give it a try for real?"

My heart flipped over in my chest. My head filled with the old memories—the roar of the ocean as it tumbled me head over heels, the harsh sand scratching my sunburned skin, the ache in my lungs as I struggled to hold my breath until I found the way back into the air again . . .

"Come on, Aves." One the whoopers, a big, hairy guy with a Mohawk, grinned at me. "You can do it."

I wasn't so sure. Floating out in the flat part of the sea was one thing, but the waves looked huge and scary, though Cam had once again assured me that they'd been smaller than usual all week. At least I thought that was what he'd said. He and his friends had all kinds of special slang for stuff, like "grommet," which I was pretty sure meant a beginner surfer.

"Let's go if we're going." Cam bent over and attached his surfboard to his leg with the little strap he'd showed me how to use yesterday. "Don't forget your leash."

I obeyed, crouching down to wrap the Velcro cuff around my ankle. Then I just stayed down there, breathing in and out and telling myself I could do this. I *had* to do it if I ever wanted to get confident enough in the ocean to swim with dolphins someday like I did in my dreams.

Cam was already halfway to the surf. He paused and looked back. "Avery!" he called. "What are you waiting for?"

"I'll let you know when I figure it out," I joked weakly.

He sighed, taking a step back toward me. Then he suddenly went all alert, like my great-uncle's hunting dog when he spotted a bird. He was looking past me now, farther up the beach.

Glancing that way myself, I saw a trio of teen-age girls in bikinis heading toward us. All three of them were carrying surfboards.

"Yo, Rachel!" Cam called, his voice suddenly a few notes deeper than usual. "What's up?"

"Cam?" I said.

He didn't seem to hear me. Or remember I was even there, actually. Kicking out of his leash, he jogged up toward the three girls, passing me without a glance.

Meanwhile, Mohawk heaved himself to his feet and grabbed his board. "That Cam does like the Bettys," he told me with a grin. "But you don't need him. Come on, just feel the wave—you'll be copacetic."

I had no idea what he was talking about. But I picked up my board and followed him toward the surf line.

There, I stopped short, watching Mohawk race into the surf with a whoop, tossing his board ahead and then belly flopping onto it. Within seconds he was paddling out past the breakers. I watched him catch a wave, leaping to his feet with surprising grace despite his size. He rode it almost all the way in before tumbling off to the side and popping up with a grin.

I couldn't help smiling at the joy on his face. I wanted to feel that. So why was I so afraid?

"I can do this," I muttered, leaning down to make sure my leash was securely fastened to the board.

Then I took a deep breath and started running, not giving myself a chance to second-guess this. Mohawk was right. I didn't need Cam. I just had to get in there and figure it out, sort of like how I'd figured out how to ride a bike years ago when my dad was too busy to teach me.

Running through the shallows was harder than it looked. I slowed down a lot after the first few steps and ended up having to turn sideways to avoid getting a faceful of salt spray when a wave broke right around me. I almost turned back then, thinking it would be better to wait a little longer to try this.

But what good would waiting do? It had already been five years since The Incident. If I ever wanted to get over it, this was my chance, and I might as well just go for it—like ripping off a Band-Aid. So I kept going, holding on tightly to my board with both hands until I was deep enough to flop onto it.

I managed to make it out past the spot where most of the waves started to swell up and then break. It was nice and calm out there, just like the day before, and I was tempted to stay, spending another pleasant morning paddling around and looking for dolphins.

But if I let myself do that, I had a feeling I'd never get over my phobia. Besides, there was no rule that said I had to stand up on my board this first time. I could just bodyboard in, like Cam had helped me do in my first lesson. That had been sort of fun. So what was the big deal?

Thinking once more of my dolphin dreams, I turned and paddled toward shore, trying to remember what Cam had told me about how to catch a wave. I was supposed to watch until I saw a promising swell, then paddle faster and catch up just before it crested. Was that right?

I glanced in at the beach. Cam was still talking to one of the girls, a pretty blonde in a red bikini.

But never mind him. I didn't need him to hold my hand. I could do this!

Spotting a promising wave, I kicked off, clutching the sides of the board tightly as I propelled myself with my feet. But I got a little crooked coming in, and when the wave lifted my board, I could feel myself turning, flipping . . .

I lost hold of my board as the wave engulfed me, tumbling me over and over. I felt the board slip out of my grip and clunk me on the shoulder and leg, but I couldn't even lift a hand to defend myself from further attacks. The wave was pulling me down, down, down, all the way to the scratchy, sandy sea floor where I'd never be able to breathe again . . .

"Avery!" a watery voice called, and a second later I felt strong hands gripping my arm and dragging me upward. At least I thought it might be upward. I was totally disoriented, my head spinning, my heart pounding, my skin raw from scraping over the sand, and my eyes burning from the salt.

It was Mohawk. He pulled me the rest of the way upright. Only then did I realize we were back on the beach, the wave that had beat me up already receding. A few seconds later the water was only ankle high.

"You okay, girl?" Mohawk asked, shooting a look toward Cam, who was completely oblivious to my wipeout. "Want me to get your cousin?"

"N-no, that's okay." I bent and detached the leash from my ankle with shaking fingers. "I'm fine."

"Cool." Mohawk gave me a little salute, then jogged back into the water with his board.

I managed to drag Cam's spare board up beyond the reach of the water. Then I did my best to shake most of the sand out of my bathing suit and hair. Feeling foolish and sore and like I might cry, I decided I'd had enough surfing for today. I left the board where it was, too shaky to carry it up the zillion steps leading up the cliff to the road. I barely made it up the steps myself. But when I reached the top, I stopped only for a second to catch my breath before heading home. Or whatever passed for "home" these days, anyway.

Mom was out in the tiny front yard when I reached the house, her cell phone pressed to her ear. She hung up as I pushed in through the gate.

"Guess what?" she sang out, her blue eyes—the exact same shade as mine—sparkling in a way I hadn't seen for a while. In fact, she looked happier and more excited than she had since the divorce. Younger, too, with her face tanned by the California sun and her hair pulled back in a ponytail.

"What?" I tried to sound happy myself, even though it wasn't easy.

Mom tucked her phone into the pocket of her seersucker shorts. "That was my lawyer. She was calling to let me know she figured out a way to free up some of the settlement money early, even though we still haven't—well, never mind all the boring details." She let out a breathless little laugh and waved one hand as if shooing away a mosquito. "The point is, we have some money again. She even said there's more than enough for a down payment if I want to start looking for a house."

"A house?" My heart jumped into my throat. "We're moving back home?"

"What? No." Mom shook her head, thrown off her happiness only for a second. "I mean a house out here in California. Isn't that exciting? We're going to be California girls for real, baby!"

She grabbed me, pulling me toward her, so close I could smell her vanilla-peach shampoo. I hugged her back, trying to hide my dismay. California girls—that was what Cam had called me, too. But that had just been a joke. We weren't really staying here forever, were we? Somehow, this was the first time I'd really thought about it. Somehow, I'd been assuming that this was temporary, that we'd be going back to our real home and our real friends as soon as everything was settled with the divorce.

Or maybe that my dad would come to his senses, and start missing us, and call us home . . .

"Ew." Mom pulled back quickly, laughing. "You're all wet and sandy!"

"Sorry. I'll go change." I hurried toward the house, glad for an excuse to hide from her while I figured out how I felt about this.

The sounds of loud chatter and shrieks of laughter met me halfway up the stairs. When I pushed open the bedroom door, Kady was in there with a couple of her friends, all three of them huddled around the little desk Kady called her vanity. They looked up with alarm, then immediately relaxed.

"Oh, it's just you." Kady hopped up and came over to kick the door shut again. "Mom's not home yet, is she?" She smirked at her friends. "I don't want her to know I borrowed some of her foundation."

"And her lipstick," one of the friends put in.

"And this amazing Chanel blush," the third girl said, dabbing some garish pink stuff on her cheeks.

"No, that's my mom's," the second girl corrected with a giggle. "She's so going to kill me if she figures out where it went . . ."

Now I noticed that they all had shiny, glittery goop on their faces. They looked ridiculous—not that I was about to tell them that.

"Didn't see Aunt Janice," I said, heading for the tiny corner of the closet Kady had grudgingly cleared for me to use. I rummaged around until I found a pair of shorts and a T-shirt. Then I headed to the bathroom to shower and change.

A few minutes later I was clean, dry, and sand-free. I dropped my sandy suit in the hamper near the laundry closet, not slowing down as I passed Kady's room. Downstairs, I headed into the den. Uncle Phil was there watching some sports show on TV.

"Hi, Avery," he said in his booming voice. Uncle Phil was loud and happy and outgoing—

the life of the party, my mom always said. Even as kids, Kady and I had noticed that our fathers were opposites in most ways—Uncle Phil big and tan and loud and always smiling; my father slight and pale and quiet and always serious.

"Hi," I said. "Do you have any binoculars I could borrow?"

"Binoculars?" He scratched his head and stood up. "Sure thing. You want to spy on the neighbors?"

I chuckled along at the lame joke. "Actually, I want to look for dolphins from up on the overlook."

"Dolphins, eh?" He stepped over to the built-in entertainment center and opened a drawer near the bottom. After scrabbling around in there for a second, he came up with a dusty pair of binoculars.

I thanked him and ducked out the back door, not wanting to run into Mom again just then. Soon I was on the ridge overlooking the north end of the beach. The sign there called it a scenic overlook, and there was a bench and a few flowers and a little metal fence to keep people from tumbling down the sheer rock face onto the sand thirty feet below. Cam and his friends usually surfed at the south end, where the waves were bigger and the beach wasn't as rocky. This end was deserted most of the time, other than the occasional old guy with a metal detector or strolling couple looking for privacy. Right now the only signs of life were a few gulls pecking at a clump of seaweed.

But I didn't look at the beach for long. I wiped the lenses of the binoculars clean, then played with them, figuring out how to adjust the focus. We'd done a whole unit on optics and lenses and stuff in my accelerated science class last year, and it was interesting to put it into practice.

Once I had the hang of it, I started scanning the water out beyond the waves, looking for anything breaking the surface.

While I looked, my mind wandered back to my wipeout, and then to what Mom had told me. Were we really going to live here now? Because so far I was a big fail when it came to being a surfing California girl . . .

Just then my gaze swept past something dark and moving, and I gasped and forgot about that other stuff. Turning back to the spot, I held my breath and waited.

It didn't take long before I saw a dorsal fin breaking into view. A dolphin! I widened my view and saw several more fins appearing and disappearing nearby.

"It's a whole pod!" I whispered with delight, all gloomy thoughts scattering immediately.

Then one of the dolphins leaped up, coming almost all the way out of the water. A second one porpoised behind it. That was what the guy at the aquarium back home had told me it was called when a dolphin jumped just above the surface while swimming fast.

I watched as the pod leaped and played, pressing the binoculars against my eye sockets so hard that I was sure I'd look like a raccoon afterward. But I didn't care. This was amazing!

Another dolphin breached, seeming to hang in the air for several seconds before splashing back down. This one looked different—darker, and oddly mottled. I stayed focused on the spot where he'd gone down, wanting a second look.

And I soon got it, as the mottled dolphin leaped up again, twisting and then diving back down with a dramatic flick of his tail. He was darker than the others, his glossy sides dusted with pale spots. I'd never seen a dolphin like that before. Was he a different kind, or just uniquely marked for some reason, like my friend Bree from back home who had so many freckles that her face looked more dark than light?

Either way, seeing him jump and play with his pod made me feel happier about life in general. Maybe I wasn't quite ready to be a California girl just yet, but at least being here meant I got to have moments like this. At least there was that.

6

Maria

I never did see the dolphins that day. But by the time I left the cove, my drawing was as good as I could get it. Seurat seemed to be alive on the page, his wet skin gleaming beneath the bright sun, his black eyes bright and curious and gazing out at me as if he knew I'd created him. Back home in my room with my sketchpad on my lap, I traced the outline of his dorsal fin with my finger, smiling as I remembered the many times I'd seen him looking just like this, full of life and happy and leaping for the sheer joy of it. I'd done my best to capture his spirit, not just the lines of his body. And I was pretty sure I'd succeeded. If I tried to do anything else now, add more detail or fix anything that didn't look perfect, I'd only make it worse. Besides that, the applications were due by the end of the week, and I didn't want to wait until the last minute. The post office was closed on Sunday, which meant I wouldn't be able to mail it today. But at least I could get everything ready so I could drop it off first thing in the morning.

The only printer in our house was in the living room. I set the sketch aside and finished filling out the application online. Then I carried my laptop down the hall with me, wanting to make sure nobody was around before starting to print. The last thing I needed right now was a lot of questions from my nosy family about what I was doing.

The house was silent—my mother always went over to her sister's house after church, usually staying until it was time to come home and start dinner. My father had left for the store half an hour ago, Josie was probably still at the beach, and as for

Nico? Well, who knew where he might be, but he usually spent as little time at home on weekends as possible, especially now that he had his driver's license and an old beat-up Toyota that he'd bought from a friend.

First I used the copier function on the printer to duplicate my drawing, since the application instructions had specified that they didn't want us to send the only copy of anything, just in case it got lost in the mail. Then I opened the laptop and scrolled down through the document, checking once more for typos or other errors. But everything looked perfect. Holding my breath, I hit the tab to print it out.

The printer was just wheezing into life, crunching and groaning like a troll awakening beneath a bridge, when I heard the front door slam open. Glancing up and over the kitchen counter, I saw my brother coming in.

He spotted me right away, even though I was trying to pretend I was invisible. "Hey, Maria." He hurried through the kitchen and under the little arch leading into the living room. "Didn't think anybody'd be home. What are you up to?"

"Nothing," I said, though the noisy printer belied what I'd said. "Um, just printing something."

"Duh." He tossed his car keys on the coffee table and came a few steps closer. "Printing what? School's out, you know."

I forced a laugh. "Yeah. Um . . ." I thought fast. I didn't want to have to explain what it was, especially since I didn't even know if I'd get in. "It's . . . an application. For . . . a job."

He looked surprised. "Job? You? You're only, what, eleven?"

"Twelve," I corrected. But even as I said it, I knew he was right. What kind of job would someone my age be applying for?

Before I could come up with another lie, the tinny chorus of a popular song burst out of Nico's shorts pocket. It was his phone, and when he pulled it out and looked at the screen, his face lit up.

"Hey, Sof," he said, pressing it to his ear without so much as another glance at me. He wandered off down the hall toward his room.

Saved by the girlfriend! I slumped with relief, then glanced at the paper now unwinding slowly, slowly out of the machine . . .

An eon or two later, it was finally finished. I turned off the printer, then grabbed the application and my laptop and scurried off to my room. I'd already set out a manila envelope, and soon my application and sketch were tucked safely inside. I addressed it, then hid it under my mattress so Josie wouldn't see it and ask any nosy questions before I mailed it out tomorrow.

That night as I slid into my usual seat at dinner, I couldn't stop thinking about the package. What would the judges think of my sketch? The rules hadn't specified topics or medium, but suddenly my black-and-white dolphin drawing seemed childish and unworthy of such a prestigious art program. Was it good enough, or was I deluding myself?

Sunday night dinners were usually a big deal at

our house. That was when my *abuelita*, my dad's mom, came over, along with her longtime helper, a tiny, grizzled woman from Panama named Aggie. My mom's sister, Tia Teresa, usually came, too, bringing her third husband and their four-year-old. Tonight Josie had brought home a couple of friends from the beach, and Nico's girlfriend, Sofia, was there, too, so the dining room was crowded and noisy, with arms reaching here and there for Mom's *albóndigas*, Teresa's noodle casserole, and the half-dozen other dishes crammed onto every spare inch of the table.

"Maria! Wake up, girl." Tia Teresa snapped her fingers in my direction. "Pass the rice, would you?"

"Sure." I grabbed the dish, almost burning my hand on the hot crockery.

After I'd passed it on, I fell back into my own thoughts. The best young artists from up and down the coast would be trying to get into the program, including a few really talented people from my school. What made me think I was special enough?

Then again, why not me? Everyone had always said I had a talent for art. Well, almost everyone. My family had never had much use for my scribbling, as my mother called it. When my grandfather was alive, he used to take me to museums now and then, once even driving us all the way down to San Diego for a special exhibit at the Museum of Contemporary Art. But the rest of them thought most art was a waste of time—time that could be spent on something more sensible, like studying hard so you'd get a good job someday, or playing sports so you'd stay in shape. Art wasn't practical, and my family was all about being practical.

But I'd been the teacher's pet of every art teacher since first grade, and I'd even won a prize for one of my paintings at the end of fifth grade. That had made even my parents pay attention, though Papa had complained that I should have won the Best Academic award, too, like Josie had a couple of years earlier.

Suddenly I heard my name and snapped out of my thoughts. Everyone was looking at me.

"Well?" Nico said with that oily grin that meant he was being a little bit mean, probably to show off for Sofia. "Will you be managing the grocery store, or running the bank, or what? You won't have much time for that chicken scratching you're always doing once you're nine-to-fiving it, you know."

"Huh?" I looked around for a hint as to what he was talking about.

"Nico, hush," my mother chided. Then she glanced at me. "Nico was just telling us you're applying for a job, Maria. What's that all about?"

"Yes, tell us." Teresa's husband chuckled, which made his spare chin jiggle. "What sorts of jobs are hiring children these days? And do they provide a 401(k)?"

I didn't know what that was, but then I was used to ignoring not-really-my-Uncle Hector and his so-called jokes that were never funny. Besides, I'd finally caught up to the conversation. Until now, the thought of what might become of my application had distracted me and made me forget that

Nico had caught me printing it out. Why had I told him that silly lie about looking for a job? Then again, what else could I have told him? Certainly not the truth—not unless I never wanted to hear the end of it . . .

"Um, it was just a—a job at that surf camp up the coast," I stammered out, hoping I didn't look as guilty and frazzled as I felt. "But I noticed at the last minute that you have to be fourteen, so I tore it up and threw it away."

"Too bad." Papa helped himself to more beans. "You're a good surfer, Maria, and I'm sure you'd be an asset to that surf camp. But never mind, maybe when you're older, eh?"

I felt a little glow at Papa's compliment. But it lasted only until my mother's next comment.

"You know, Maria, Josie was already baby-sitting by the time she was your age," she said. "If you're looking for some spending money, you could ask around with the neighbors."

"That's a great idea," Tia Teresa agreed. She patted her son, who was busy sticking a green bean up his nose. "If I decide to go back to work, you'll be the first person I call to watch little Oscar."

With some effort, I managed not to shudder at the thought. "It's okay," I told my mother. "I don't really need a job, I just thought—"

"No, Mom's right," Josie interrupted. "I can ask around with my old clients if you want, *chica*."

"That's a good idea, Josie." Papa beamed at her, looking as proud as if his middle child had just announced that she'd discovered the cure for the common cold. "You do that."

"No," I said, but nobody was listening to me anymore. They were all chattering at one another about people they knew with kids, how young people weren't willing to work hard for what they had anymore, and how the kids from this family would never be so spoiled as that, *Dios mediante*.

And just like that, my fictional job search had become a family project. All I could do was finish eating as quickly as possible. Luckily it was Josie's turn to clear, so I was able to rush down to the cove for some thinking space, leaving the house in such a hurry that I forgot both my board and my sketchpad.

But that was okay. My application drawing was finished, and as soon as I saw Seurat's familiar spotted face poking up out of the water, I remembered that it was good, maybe even good enough to get me into that art program. If it did, I could deal with my family and their jobs and comments later.

Feeling better already, I pushed through the breakers, which were bigger now than earlier, and waded out to the drop-off. I stood there for a long time with the cool water swirling around my waist, just watching the dolphins. Seurat hung back, not seeming to be in the mood to show off this evening. But the others leaped and played and were happy and free just like always. And, just like always, they made me feel a little happier and freer, too.

7

Avery

After dinner on Sunday night, I walked back out
to the ridge with the binoculars slung around my
neck on their nylon cord. It wouldn't be dark for at
least an hour yet, and Mom and Aunt Janice were
chattering nonstop about Realtors and square
footage and stuff while they cleaned up the kitchen.
Even Kady seemed interested in the house-hunting
project. She'd volunteered to go with them to look
at places, actually sounding excited about it.

Mom had glanced at me when Kady said that,
clearly expecting me to chime in. But I'd taken a
big gulp of my water to avoid having to speak.

I still wasn't sure what to think about living here permanently. Actually, I was trying not to think about it at all. I was just a kid—that meant I didn't have much say about stuff like that. So why stress myself out?

The scenic overlook was deserted, as usual, although a handful of high school kids were wandering along the beach at the surf line just below. They didn't look up, though, and I ignored them.

I scanned the ocean. At first I didn't see anything much out there. A huge ship was floating along on the horizon, though it was so far away I couldn't see much detail even with the binoculars.

There still wasn't anything happening in the waters closer in, so I focused the binoculars on the south end of the beach to see if any of Cam's friends were there. A bunch of people were on the sand or playing at the edge of the water, but nobody was surfing just then. Or were they? Spotting movement, I zoomed in on a spot beyond the end of the beach.

But it wasn't a surfer I'd seen—it was that black-and-white spotted dolphin! I was just in time to see him seem to pop out of the cliffs at the edge of the sea. He only stayed at the surface briefly before diving back down. I waited for him to reappear or for the rest of the pod to show up. But the ocean was as still as if the dolphin had never been there.

I scanned slowly back and forth, wondering where he'd gone—and where he'd come from. When I looked more closely, I noticed a break in the cliffs stretching up from the foamy waves. Was that a cave? Or maybe some kind of cove? A second later I let out a gasp as several dolphins leaped into view, swimming out of the dark entrance to whatever-it-was.

Even after they disappeared, I fiddled with the binoculars, trying to get a better look. But it was no use. The mystery spot wasn't very far away, but it was at just the wrong angle to see anything clearly.

Letting the binoculars dangle around my neck,

I looked that way with just my eyes, trying to figure out exactly how far that cove—or whatever—might be from here. Not far, I decided. Definitely close enough to walk.

I hadn't explored my new neighborhood much yet, other than the beach and the overlook. But I knew that the main part of town was in that direction—south, just past the end of the beach. It only took me ten minutes or so to get there by walking down Overlook Avenue, the two-lane road that wound its way along the shoreline. The town was pretty small, with just a couple of traffic lights on Center Street. That was the main street, although it wasn't much of one. There were mostly just more houses, although they were bigger and older than the ones in my aunt and uncle's neighborhood. Clustered on the two or three blocks nearest the ocean were a few small stores, a bank, a post office, and the police station. Most people did their shopping on the big highway a few miles inland, or at least that was what Aunt Janice had told us when we arrived. That was where the mall was, and the grocery store, and all the other normal stuff.

It was Sunday, so even the few little shops were closed for the evening by then. The only exception was the fancy seafood restaurant perched on a cliff overlooking the ocean where Aunt Janice and the others had taken Mom and me for dinner on our first night in California. People were hanging around on the sidewalk outside staring at their cell phones, and jangly music drifted toward me on the breeze blowing in off the water. But nobody looked my way as I crossed Center Street and kept going.

For another block or two, the neighborhood looked pretty much the same as the one where my aunt and uncle lived. But after that, things started to change. The houses got smaller, and there were a few apartment buildings mixed in. Some of the houses were nice, with brightly painted shutters and flowers in the yard, but others looked a little run-down.

Then I passed another restaurant, this one with

part of the sign in Spanish. Lively music was coming out of this place, and a woman heading toward the door cast me a curious look as she passed. The bright neon lights of the signs advertising Coca-Cola lit up the sidewalk and made me realize it was getting dark already. I was tempted to turn back but couldn't resist going a little farther.

At the next corner, I took a few steps down the little half block between Overlook Avenue and the ocean. I couldn't tell how high up I was right now, or if this was far enough to start looking for that cove I'd seen. When I reached the end of the street, I could see that I hadn't gone far enough yet.

"Hey, you!" a shout came from behind me.

Turning, I saw a pair of boys a little older than me riding bikes. They pedaled closer, doing wheelies along the way, both of them grinning and staring at me.

"What you doing here, *blanquita*?" one of the boys demanded, doing another wheelie while his friend circled nearby.

"Yeah, you lost?" The second boy added something in Spanish that made the first boy laugh.

I stepped to the side, dodging past them. "I was just leaving," I muttered, though I'm not sure they heard me.

"Don't be scared!" one of the boys called after me. "You never seen a good-looking Latino before?"

That made both of them laugh again. I sped up, afraid they might follow me, but their laughter faded quickly into the distance. Still, I didn't slow down or look back until I'd crossed Center Street.

When I let myself into the house, Cam and Kady were in the den arguing over what to watch on TV.

"Where've you been?" Cam asked. "I thought you were upstairs."

"Just walking." I perched on the edge of the sofa. "Actually, I was looking for a cave I saw."

"A cave?" Kady wrinkled her nose. "What are you talking about?"

"Maybe it's a cove," I corrected. "Anyway, it's south of the beach—I saw it through the binoculars, so I walked over that way to see if I could find it."

"South?" Kady sat up a little straighter. "How far south?"

"Past Center Street, I don't know how far. Five or six blocks, maybe?"

"Oh." Cam traded a look with his sister. "You probably shouldn't go down that way, Avery."

"Why not?" I asked.

Kady was making a face as if she smelled something bad. "I heard there are gangs there and stuff."

I flashed back briefly to those two boys on bikes. They'd been kind of obnoxious, but I couldn't imagine them as part of a gang. At least not the type I'd seen in the movies.

"Really?" I asked, glancing over at Cam.

He flicked through a couple of channels with the remote, keeping his eyes on the TV. "I don't know about gangs," he said.

"Yes, there are," Kady insisted, frowning at him and grabbing the remote out of his hand.

"You shouldn't go near that part of town. It's bad news."

When I looked at Cam again, he shrugged. "It's probably better to stay on this side of Center," he said. "Just in case."

"Okay," I said.

But I didn't mean it. I couldn't stop thinking about how the black-and-white dolphin and all his friends had come swimming out through that opening. If I could find the cove, or cave, or whatever it was, maybe I'd be able to see them up close! And that neighborhood hadn't seemed so bad. Just . . . different.

So the next morning after breakfast, I went out searching again. The seafood restaurant was closed at that hour on a Monday morning, and so was the Mexican place, though an old man was sweeping the sidewalk outside.

"*Hola*," he greeted me with a pleasant smile.

I smiled back, then hurried on. Soon I passed the street where I'd seen the boys the night before, and a couple of blocks later the street sloped upward and the houses on the ocean side ended. Now there were only big rocks, scrubby little trees, and spiky grass on that side, stretching toward an ocean I could no longer see thanks to the rising wall of stone.

Now what? I stopped and studied the rugged landscape, wondering if there could be a way down into that cove from here. I was pretty sure this had to be around the right area . . .

Hearing someone coming, I turned and saw a girl jogging toward me, arms and legs pumping. She was probably a year or two older than me, slim and fit and pretty with a sleek dark ponytail.

When she saw me, she slowed to a walk and plucked earbuds out of her ears. "Hi," she said. "You okay? You look lost."

I smiled weakly, ready to make an excuse and turn back. But the girl seemed friendly, and I really wanted to find out where those dolphins had come from.

"Um, I'm looking for a cove? I think?" I said uncertainly. "I mean, that's how it looked from farther up the shore. It's like an opening in the cliff, leading into the ocean?"

She nodded. "I think I know where you mean. My little sister hangs out there all the time."

I couldn't help a flash of disappointment. Somehow, I'd imagined finding a secret, private place where I could spend time with the dolphins all on my own, watching them as much as I wanted. I hadn't pictured a place with a bunch of little kids hanging around. But maybe that was silly. This was busy, crowded California, and there didn't seem to be many secret places around anywhere.

The girl was stepping past me, pointing to a worn spot in the sandy ground between two gnarled evergreens. "That's the trail in," she said. "Be careful—it's pretty steep, and nobody will be able to hear you if you fall or something once you're down there."

That sounded a little ominous, but I thanked her and moved a few steps toward the spot she'd indicated. She waved and jogged away, sticking her earbuds back in as she ran.

I stood there for a moment in the scant shade cast by the small trees. Then I started picking my way along the trail, which quickly plunged steeply down through a crevice in the rock. Halfway down, I was wishing I'd put on sneakers instead of flip-flops that morning. The trail was just as steep as the girl had warned, and narrow and rocky, too.

But I forgot all that when I emerged at the bottom. Before me lay a gorgeous cove, bigger than I'd expected, surrounded by high, dark, stone walls that shaded part of the water. Waves splashed rhythmically against a rocky beach, and a narrow outlet showed only a tiny peek of the sea beyond. And there were the dolphins!

I gasped as one of the creatures leaped out, twisting as he came down with a splash. Several dorsal fins were visible nearby, and as I watched, the black-and-white dolphin poked his head into view, seeming to smile at me as I stood there stunned by the beautiful sight. The dolphins were so close—not as close as at the aquarium, of course, but without the thick glass between us. It was amazing!

It took a good few minutes before I realized I wasn't alone. When I looked down for a second, trying to remember if I had my cell phone with me so I could take pictures, I saw a flash of color at the edge of the beach.

A girl was sitting there, so still she might have been made of stone herself. My eyes widened as I recognized her. It was the girl from the bookstore! I remembered how she'd been holding that dolphin book when I first saw her.

Then I remembered something else. Kady had told me this girl was bad news—that her brother was in a gang, and her sister was no good, either . . . I gulped, wondering if I'd just gotten myself in big trouble . . .

8

Maria

I recognized her right away. It had been almost a week since that day at the mall, but the Anglo girl looked enough like Kady Swanson that my heart skipped a beat when she walked into the cove. For a second I was sure my secret, sacred place was ruined—that obnoxious Kady and her screeching minions would be there all the time from now on, taunting me and scaring away the dolphins and talking smack about my family. The thought was unbearable, especially now, only minutes after I'd left my package at the post office as if it were just another ordinary piece of mail, like a birthday card or the water bill.

But this girl, the dolphin girl, didn't even say anything. She sent an uncertain, wavery little smile my way and then turned to look out at the dolphins again. That was good. I looked out at the water myself, just in time to see Seurat leap up three times in a row.

I couldn't help smiling at that. He was such a show-off! It was almost as if he realized there was someone new in the cove, someone who might not realize he was the greatest dolphin in the entire Pacific . . .

Still smiling, I glanced toward the other girl and caught her peeking back at me. I turned away quickly, aiming my unsmiling back in her direction. Maybe she wasn't Kady Swanson, but I didn't want to encourage her to stay, either.

But she stayed despite that. When I didn't hear her leaving, I couldn't resist sneaking another look over my shoulder. The dolphin girl had sat down cross-legged on the beach, not even seeming to care that her fancy pale-beige shorts were getting damp and probably dirty from the dark seaweedy muck that always washed up there. She had her elbows on her knees and her chin on her palm and was staring raptly out at the pod.

I closed my eyes and clutched the sketchpad in my lap, wondering what to do. Didn't this girl have anything better to occupy herself with on a sunny Monday morning than invading my favorite place? What if she brought her friend-sister-cousin-whatever Kady back here? It was hard to imagine Kady at the cove, so close to my house. So close to Josie, her sworn enemy ever since the time two years earlier when Josie won the last spot on the middle school soccer team instead of her. She hadn't liked any of us much before that, but ever since she treated us like dirt beneath her fancy name-brand shoes. So what if Josie was a year older and had played soccer since she was little, while Kady had just decided she wanted to do it that year? Kady Swanson was used to getting what she wanted, and woe befall anyone who stood in her way.

"Whoa!" the dolphin girl exclaimed, jolting me out of my unhappy memories. Seurat had just made an especially dramatic leap, and when I glanced back, the girl was grinning from ear to ear.

This time I didn't look away when she caught my eye. I even smiled a little. What was the harm in her being here? She wasn't Kady. I felt confident that Kady wouldn't smile and exclaim like that over a dolphin's leap.

But I would. And so would this girl. So maybe it was okay that she'd found her way here—at least this once.

9

Avery

I went back the next day, of course. How could I resist? I'd had my dream again, only this time the black-and-white dolphin was there with the others, swimming around with me like I was part of the pod.

The other girl was already in the cove when I arrived. This time she was standing on the beach with a battered old army-green canvas backpack at her feet. When she heard me coming, she looked around quickly and then bent to shove something back into the bag.

The girl didn't say anything, which wasn't a surprise. She hadn't said a word the whole time I was there yesterday. Well, okay, that wasn't quite true. When I'd realized I needed to get home for lunch before my mom sent out a search party, I'd said good-bye, and she'd said it back. But that was it. She didn't say anything now, or look especially happy to see me as I picked my way carefully over the last few rocky feet of trail.

I was never a big fan of silence, though. That was why my dad used to joke that I'd talk to the wall if there was nobody else around.

"Hi," I said, stepping toward her and almost tripping over some loose stones in the sand. "I'm Avery."

For a second I thought she wasn't going to respond. But finally she tipped her head forward a little.

"Maria," she said, her voice so quiet I leaned forward. "The dolphins aren't here right now."

Glancing out, I saw that she was right. The

water in the cove was undisturbed, rolling quietly in with each steady wave after wave.

"Oh," I said, disappointed. "Um, do they come here a lot?"

She looked out at the water, then back at me. "Yeah, I guess." Her voice was even softer than before. "Nobody knows except me, though."

And now me, I thought but didn't say.

I stepped forward to stand beside her, scanning the waves. "I love dolphins," I said. "That's what I started to tell you—you know, that day in the bookstore?"

She flinched, as if surprised. Had she forgotten about our first meeting?

"I wasn't sure you remembered," she said. "I mean, Kady dragged you away so fast . . ."

"You know my cousin?" I blurted out.

"She's your cousin? I figured it was something like that." Her tone and expression were vaguely disapproving. No wonder. Kady had acted like kind of a jerk that day.

"Yeah, sorry about her," I said. "She used to be cool, but now my mom says she's becoming an obnoxious teenager." I laughed, the sound bouncing off the high stone walls.

Maria barely cracked a smile. "Okay," she said.

"How do you know her? Are you in her class at school?" I asked.

Maria shook her head. "She's a year ahead of me."

"Really?" I said. "Hey, then we must be in the same grade."

"Where do you go to school?" She barely sounded interested as she stared out at the water.

"Nowhere," I said without thinking.

That made her turn and stare at me. "You don't go to school?"

I let out a nervous little laugh. "No, I do. Um, I mean, I did. Uh . . ." I swallowed hard, trying not to think about Mom's big news about the house and what that meant. Like that I might never see my friends back home again. "I mean, we just moved out here—my mom and me, that is," I explained, kicking off my flip-flops and walking over to cool my toes in the surf. "We, um, we're living with my aunt and her family for a while."

I didn't feel like talking about the divorce. Luckily Maria didn't ask any questions about what I'd just said even though it probably sounded kind of weird.

"So you're living with Kady now, huh?"

"Yeah." I shrugged. "It's bizarre, though. I hadn't seen her in like four years—that's the last time her family came out to visit. She's changed so much since then . . ." Letting my voice trail off, I traced patterns in the wet sand with my big toe.

"I know," Maria said after a moment. "I remember she used to be nicer. Or at least not so mean."

Did everyone at Maria's school think Kady was mean? If so, maybe it was just as well that my cousin was a grade ahead of me. And that she didn't seem that excited about hanging out together.

"Anyway, sorry again about how she acted at the mall," I said, turning to face Maria. "I promise I'm not like that."

She didn't answer. She was staring out toward the water again, her dark eyes suddenly bright with interest. When I turned to follow her gaze, I gasped.

"The dolphins are here!" I exclaimed.

Maria shot me a glance, a nod, and a tiny smile. Then she turned to watch the dolphins again, and so did I. At least four or five of them were zipping through the water, occasionally jumping up into view. Then another dolphin leaped up, and I smiled.

"Hey, that funny one is with them again," I exclaimed. "The black-and-white one—see? He's all spotted."

"I know. I call him Seurat." Maria sounded a little friendlier now.

"*Sir-ah*?" I imitated the way she'd said the unfamiliar name. "What's that mean?"

"Seurat, S-E-U-R-A-T. He was a painter—he invented pointillism. Do you know what that is?"

I shook my head. "What is it?"

"It's a style of painting where the artist uses only tiny dots of color, so up close the painting just looks like random spots, but from far away they combine to look like a whole scene or whatever."

That sounded familiar. "I think I saw a painting like that once," I said. "It was on a school field trip to this art museum in Chicago."

"Really? Chicago?" Maria sounded excited. "Was it a painting of people standing on the shore of a lake, ladies with parasols, stuff like that?"

"I think so." I was struggling to recall what the painting had looked like. All I could remember was my teacher, Ms. Jarvis, droning on about how many dots of paint it had taken to create this masterpiece, blah-de-blah-blah. I'd been much more interested in the candy one of my friends was passing out behind the teacher's back.

"That's amazing that you saw it in person!" She gazed at me, her eyes wide and impressed. "It's probably the most famous work of pointillism there is—and one of the most famous paintings, period."

"Yeah," I said uncertainly. "Um, I don't remember what it was called or anything, though."

"*A Sunday on La Grande Jatte*," she reeled off as easily as someone might give out their address. "By Georges-Pierre Seurat."

I looked out at the dolphins just in time to see the spotted one leap up again. "Seurat," I said. "Like our friend out there."

Maria looked really pretty when she smiled for real, instead of keeping her face all tight and wary. "Yeah. Now you see why I call him that, right?" she said.

"Sure." I smiled back. "So are you really into art, or what? I mean, most kids our age don't know much about, you know, pointillist painters and stuff. At least, I sure don't!"

She shrugged, looking away. "I guess. And you're really into dolphins, huh?"

"They're my favorite animal." I took another step into the water, hardly believing I was really here, with real dolphins just a few yards away. "I've always loved them, ever since I can remember. I might even want to become a marine biologist someday so I can study them."

"Really?" Maria said. "Well, then you probably already realized that Seurat isn't a regular bottlenose dolphin like the others."

"Oh. I guess I hadn't really thought about it." I watched as the black-and-white dolphin surfaced again, seeming to smile at us. "What is he, then?"

"I'm pretty sure he's a species called a pantropical spotted dolphin," she said. "I looked it up, and he looks just like some photos I found online. The thing is, that species isn't really native around here, but I guess sometimes they travel out of their area."

I watched one of the gray dolphins do a flip. "The rest are bottlenoses, though, right?"

"Uh-huh." She nodded. "I read that sometimes a pod will accept a dolphin of another species as one of their own. I guess that's what happened with Seurat."

"Cool." I smiled at her. "You know a lot about dolphins! Maybe you should be a marine biologist, too."

"I don't think so," she said quickly. "I'm not really into science and math and those kinds of things."

"So what are you into? Art?" I guessed again, since she hadn't really answered the first time.

"Uh-huh." She glanced down at the sand, looking shy. "Art and books, mostly."

"That's cool." I meant it, too. Maria was turning out to be a lot more interesting than she'd seemed at first, back when she wasn't talking. "You know, you're really not like I expected," I blurted out impulsively.

"What?" She turned to stare at me. "How do you mean—what were you expecting?"

I shrugged, feeling sheepish for thinking out loud, as I tended to do way too often for my own good. "I don't know, it's nothing," I said with a little laugh. "I mean, it's just some stuff that Kady and Cam told me . . ."

"What?" She'd gone all stiff again, that wary look back in her eyes. "What did they tell you about me?"

"Just that you live in, um, a bad part of town. Kady said there are some gangs in your neighborhood . . ."

"And you believed her." Maria's voice was cold now. She turned away and stared at the dolphins. "I should have known you weren't that different after all."

"What?" I frowned. "I'm not like Kady, if that's what you're saying."

She shrugged without looking my way. "You sure don't seem that different to me," she muttered. "Anyway, I have to go."

"Maria, wait . . ." I wasn't sure whether to be annoyed or embarrassed or mad or what. But it didn't matter. She'd already grabbed her bag and scurried off up the trail without looking back.

10

Maria

I woke up on Thursday morning thinking about the art program submission. Until then, I'd managed to put it out of my mind, at least mostly, by telling myself that I needed to be patient and allow time for the package to get there, then picturing it swimming slowly along through the US postal system like a salmon migrating back to its faraway breeding grounds. But overnight, my subconscious had decided that enough time had passed, and that I could start worrying now.

As I brushed my teeth, I stared at myself in the mirror. It was still partly steamed over from Nico's shower, making me look like a ghost or an impressionist painting, with big, blurry, nervous eyes and wavery, watery frown lines across my forehead. It was weird to imagine the judges, a bunch of strangers, poring over the drawing I'd worked so hard on down at the cove. Would they think it was too simple, too childish? Or would they like it? How soon would I have an answer?

I jumped as someone pounded on the bathroom door. "Maria!" Josie called. "Are you in there?"

"Yeah, I'm almost finished." I spit out the last minty mouthful of toothpaste, then let myself out of the bathroom. I was dressed in my swimsuit and one of Papa's baggy old T-shirts as a cover-up, ready to head down to the cove. I hadn't gone there yesterday, mostly because I didn't want to run into that Avery girl again. But I needed the dolphins right now to help me take my mind off what might be happening with my submission. Watching them always made me feel better about everything.

Josie was waiting in the hallway, looking impatient. "Guess what?" she said. "I found you a job!"

"What?" I'd all but forgotten about Sunday night's dinner conversation, mostly because my family hadn't mentioned it since. Then again, I'd barely seen them over the past few days—my parents had been busy at work, Nico had spent most of his time with Sofia as usual, and Josie had dashed in and out being social and popular and far too busy to hang out with her boring little sister.

"It's a babysitting gig." Josie looked pleased with herself, the lopsided dimples in her cheeks staring at me like dark little extra eyes. "Mrs. Vargas just told me the boys' grandmother is going on a cruise for like half the summer, and they need someone who can come three times a week while she's away."

"The Vargas twins?" I shuddered at the thought of the two little boys, probably around three now, who lived a couple of blocks away. I knew them—everyone in the neighborhood knew them. There was no way to avoid noticing those twin whirlwinds of yelling and destructive energy who left nothing but chaos in their wake.

My sister nodded. "I know they're a handful, but the Vargases pay really well," she assured me. "I'd take the job myself if I had time."

Sure she would. Nobody in their right mind would take that job if they had any other choice at all. Not if they wanted to stay sane, with all their limbs intact.

"So what do you say?" She was sounding impatient again, probably because I'd been struck dumb with shock at the very notion that I'd voluntarily submit myself to spending time with the Vargas twins. "Sounds perfect, right?"

"I don't know . . . I'm not sure I really want to work that much this summer after all," I said.

"It's only three days a week," Josie said again, a little slower this time just in case I'd suddenly gone deaf or stupid. "Anyway, what else do you have to do? You can't spend all your time hanging around in that cove of yours."

That showed what she knew. Restless, always active Josie would never be able to understand why I spent so much time at the cove. To her, watching dolphins for more than thirty seconds would probably be boring and a good reason to go for a run or rustle up a pickup game of beach volleyball. How could we be sisters and yet so different?

I was tempted to tell her about the art program. Maybe that would get her off my back, impress her a little. She was competitive—if she knew I was waiting to hear back from such a selective place, would she see why I couldn't be distracted by the Vargas twins right now? Maybe she'd even agree to keep the news from Mom and Papa. Then again, maybe not . . .

"Seriously, Maria," she said before I could decide what to say. "I went out of my way to set this up for you. The least you can do is go talk to Mrs. Vargas this afternoon when she gets home, okay? She's expecting you at four thirty."

She stomped away, leaving me with my mouth hanging open and my protests still stuck in my throat.

Twenty minutes later, I was picking my way down the cove trail with my surfboard under my arm. Something felt different about the air today, and even before I made the last twisting turn, I knew what I would see when the beach came into view.

Sure enough, Avery was there, perched on a rock and staring out at the water. She turned when she heard me coming.

"Maria!" she exclaimed, rushing to meet me as I stepped over the last of the big rocks and dropped my board on the sand. "I'm so glad you're here. I'm really, really sorry about the other day, okay?"

I blinked at her, not prepared to deal with this at the moment. "Um, what?"

"I mean it—I was totally out of line." She clutched her hands together and gazed at me with big, puppy-dog eyes the same shade of blue as the sunlit shallows nearby. "I shouldn't have listened to crazy Kady, and I shouldn't have said that stuff about you and your neighborhood and your brother and everything." She smiled tentatively. "Please say you'll forgive me? I really want to be friends again."

"Friends?" I echoed. "I didn't realize that's what we were."

She laughed breathlessly. "Funny! So do you forgive me?"

I shrugged with one shoulder, which she seemed to take as a yes. She laughed again, then waved toward the water. "I haven't seen the dolphins yet today," she said. "They were here yesterday, though."

She'd been here yesterday? That figured. I had the sinking feeling I was never going to be rid of this girl, whether I liked it or not. Couldn't she see that we had nothing in common? Well, nothing except the dolphins, anyway. And that just didn't seem like enough.

Wanting to escape those thoughts—and her— I kicked off my shoes and peeled off Papa's shirt. "I need a swim," I said, heading for the water. As I waded into the shallows, jumping a little every few steps to avoid the gently breaking waves trying to splash salt spray into my eyes and nose, I thought

I saw a dorsal fin breaking the surface out near the mouth of the cove. The dolphins were here, which made me feel somehow superior, as if they'd waited for my arrival to show up.

"Maria!" Avery called from behind me. "Hold on, are you . . ."

I dived in at the drop-off, and the rest of whatever she was saying was lost in the gurgling sound of water rushing past my ears. I stayed under as long as I could, finally emerging about halfway out into the cove. Treading water, I glanced back and saw that Avery had followed me in, though she was only a few yards beyond the beach. Blinking the moisture out of my eyes, I realized she was clutching my battered old striped surfboard.

"Hey," I muttered, too quietly for her to hear. "Did I say you could borrow that?"

She took another step and suddenly plunged down, letting out a little shriek of surprise at the sudden drop-off. My board went flying and I rolled my eyes and turned away, wondering if I'd ever have the cove to myself again.

Avery

Panic grabbed me as my foot disappeared into nothingness. Where had the sea floor gone? I tried to step back, but it was too late. My arms windmilled, and a second later my chin slipped below the surface. Salty water filled my mouth and nose.

"Urgh!" I gurgled, spitting and doing my best to tread water. I'd lost my grip on Maria's surfboard, and it was floating uselessly a couple of yards away—though it might as well have been a couple of miles. Why, oh why had I decided to try to follow Maria in to make sure she wasn't still mad? I should have waited until she returned to shore. I'd thought I could get on the surfboard before the water got too deep, but I didn't expect it to get so deep so quickly. Still, I tried to tell myself that it was no biggie—that this was no different from the deep end of the community pool back home, where I used to swim all the time.

Just then a swell rolled by, lifting me up and making my stomach lurch like I was on a roller coaster. It was no use. This was way different from being in a pool, and I knew it. I wished I was back on the safe, dry beach. What if it was too rough for me to get back there? What if a wave tumbled me around, with no Uncle Phil or Mohawk guy to rescue me this time?

"Help!" I yelled, except it came out in a tiny squeak that would never carry all the way out to where Maria was floating, her back to me, oblivious to what was happening. Why wouldn't she turn around?

My head pounded and my limbs felt cold and heavy. Once again my chin slipped under, and this time some of the salty water went down my throat and made me cough. I fought my way back to the air, gasping like a fish, but my lungs were too tight with panic to suck in anything but a little sea spray. Another wave pushed at me, and I felt myself sinking again despite my thrashing arms and legs . . .

Then I felt something nudge me. Looking down, I gasped and swallowed another mouthful of water. It was Seurat!

The dolphin seemed much larger up close. I probably should have been afraid—here I was, trapped in the rough sea with a wild animal!—but somehow I knew it was okay. He was there to help. Just being this close to him brought me a little flash of the feeling from my dreams, and that made me feel calmer right away. Seurat floated close beside me, still nudging me toward shore, not seeming to mind when I tentatively slid my palm over his side. Once again I couldn't breathe, but this time it was from awe. He felt warm and solid and wet and smooth—well, mostly smooth, anyway. I paused in surprise as I felt a weird lump on his torso . . .

"Avery!" Maria shouted from somewhere behind me. Just like that, Seurat slipped underwater and away, disappearing as if he'd never been there. "Avery, are you okay?"

Then she was beside me, dragging her surfboard along with her. She helped me grab onto the board, hoisting me partway on and then pulling me along toward shore. The waves splashed over us, but Maria steadied the board and I stayed upright.

I'd never been so glad to put my bare feet down on gritty, rocky sand. Maria dropped the surfboard at the edge of the water and guided me over to sit on a big rock back by the cliffs.

"What was that all about?" she exclaimed, sinking onto another rock nearby. "*Híjole!* It looked like you were drowning or something!" Then she shot me a sidelong look. "And was Seurat helping you?"

"I—I think so." I heaved a deep breath, still feeling awed by the close encounter with the spotted dolphin. "I think he knew I was freaking out and came to rescue me."

"Hmm." Maria was silent for a long moment. "I've read about stuff like that—dolphins rescuing swimmers in trouble." Then she frowned. "Why were you in trouble, anyway? The water was perfectly calm."

"Oh." I bit my lip, feeling embarrassed. "Um, I just didn't realize it dropped off like that. When you dived in, I figured it was just because you were tired of wading."

"So what if it dropped off? You can swim, can't you?"

"Of course!" I said quickly. I slid my eyes toward her, wondering if she was going to make fun of me if she heard the truth. "The thing is, I'm, um . . ."

"What?" She didn't sound accusing or judgmental. Just confused.

"I'm a little bit afraid of the ocean." It came out in a rush, and she frowned slightly, maybe not sure she'd heard me right. "It started when I came out to visit about five years ago . . ."

I told her the whole story, including the part where I wouldn't go anywhere near the water for the rest of that trip, and how my parents made me take tons of swimming lessons once we were back home. Only it obviously hadn't really helped me get over my fear, not even now that I was older.

"Wow," Maria said when I told her about my pathetic attempt at surfing last weekend. "Good thing that guy was there to pull you out."

"Yeah. And it's a good thing you were here to help me today." I shot her an only-slightly-shaky smile. "Thanks."

"You're welcome." She smiled back, her dark eyes friendlier now. "But it looked like Seurat had things all under control."

"Yeah." I shivered at the memory of running my hand over the dolphin's body. "Actually, that's the main reason I wanted to learn to swim in the ocean."

"What is?"

I hesitated, shooting her another look. I'd never told anyone about my dreams before. They were just too private, too special. But for some reason, I had a feeling this girl might understand.

"It's because of dolphins," I said. "See, I've been having this amazing dream my whole life where I'm out in the ocean, swimming with a bunch of dolphins, and it's like the best thing ever. I always feel really good when I wake up afterward—like I can do anything, you know?"

She was quiet for a few seconds, staring out at the water. There were a few dolphins swimming around, though I couldn't see Seurat just then.

"That sounds really special," she said at last.

"It is." I nodded vigorously. "So that's why I wanted Cam to teach me to surf. Only I'm not sure he was ready for a nervous student like me. I sort of felt like I was in the way, even though I don't think he meant to make me feel like that." I grimaced. "Unlike a certain other cousin of mine, who goes out of her way to let me know I'm in her way . . ."

"Kady." It wasn't really a question, more like an answer.

"Yeah." I picked at a rough spot on the rock beside me. "Sorry again about listening to all her stupid lies about you and your family. I should've known better."

"There aren't really any gangs in my neighborhood." Maria made a face. "Although goofy Manny Aguilar and his friends like to pretend they're tough sometimes."

I laughed. "I knew some guys like that back home," I said. "They were ridiculous."

Just then one of the dolphins leaped extra high, splashing down in a spray of foam. "Wow," Maria said with a smile. "I bet Seurat will jump even higher now. He doesn't like to see the others show off more than him."

I giggled, glad that things were friendly between us again. But her mention of Seurat reminded me of something.

"Hey," I said. "When Seurat was helping me, I felt something weird."

"What do you mean?" She was still smiling, watching the dolphins play.

"It was a lump, sort of on his side or stomach." I pointed to my own stomach to illustrate.

She turned to face me. "What kind of lump?"

"It felt . . ." I hesitated, trying to figure out how to describe it. "Um, one of my friends back home had this big old black Lab. He started getting these big, round lumps on his chest, and when they took him to the vet, it turned out it was cancer."

Alarm flashed in Maria's dark eyes. "Cancer? I'm sure whatever you felt was nothing like that."

"Probably not," I agreed. "Seurat's lump felt bigger than the ones that dog had."

"Yeah. Plus, you were panicking, so who knows if—well, anyway." She stood up, brushing sand off her hands. "Hey, I have an idea."

I could tell she was trying to change the subject. That was fine with me. She was probably right—I'd never even touched a dolphin before. Whatever I'd felt on the dolphin's body, it couldn't be anything bad. Not when Seurat was so amazing and full of life.

"What?" I asked.

"You said you feel weird having your cousin and his friends trying to teach you to surf," she said. "Well, maybe you'd feel less weird about me teaching you?" She waved a hand toward the water. "Here, where it's private."

"Really?" I was kind of amazed that she was offering to teach me. To be honest, I'd had the feeling she didn't even want me around. Maybe we really were becoming friends! "Sure, thanks! That would be great." I hesitated. "There's no lifeguard here, though, is there?"

The question sounded stupid even as I said it. What, did I think there was a lifeguard hidden behind that craggy rock over there? Or perched up on the cliff wall, staring down at us with binoculars? But Maria just shook her head.

"No lifeguard except me," she said. "If you don't think your mom would let you . . ."

"No, it's okay," I said quickly. Mom hadn't really told me everything about this move, after all—like that it would be permanent. So what was the harm if I didn't tell her everything about my surfing lessons? I was sure Cam wouldn't even notice I wasn't at his beach anymore, and Mom would probably be too busy house hunting to ask me too many questions.

Maria nodded, watching me. "You'll be okay," she said. "The water's always really calm here, and I've been swimming since before I could walk. Besides," she added with a smile, "I have Seurat to help me keep an eye on you, right?"

"Right!" All my worries fled at the memory of touching the dolphin. "Okay, then it's a deal—as long as you don't mind how nervous and remedial I am."

"I don't mind." She stepped over and picked up her surfboard. "I mean, you can swim a little, right?"

"Sure! I think it's just the waves that freak me

out." I stood and followed her toward the water's edge. "I can swim just fine in a pool."

I felt a jangle of nerves as soon as I stepped foot in the cold water. But I did my best to ignore that, letting Maria talk me through some surfing basics. She was a surprisingly good teacher, and the waves really were pretty small compared to the ones on the main beach. I had a few moments of panic, but before I knew it, she had me bodyboarding without wiping out once.

It helped that the dolphins hung around to watch, although I didn't see Seurat again that day. Seeing them out there reminded me why I was doing this—it wasn't just because surfing seemed like so much fun; it was also a way to get over my fears and maybe make my dolphin dreams come true someday. And now, for the first time, with Maria's help, I was starting to think that could actually happen.

12

Maria

On Friday morning, I was sitting cross-legged on the beach working on a sketch of a dragonfly when I heard grunts and clunks from above. I stuck my pad and pencil in my bag and stepped to the bottom of the trail. There was Avery, struggling down the narrow trail with a well-worn blue surfboard.

"Whoa," she said with a laugh when she saw me. "And I thought it was tough getting down here without this thing!"

"You'll get used to it." I wasn't sure whether to be glad or not-so-glad that she'd come again so soon. She'd done fairly well the day before—she was a fast learner, and pretty athletic, and she really could swim just fine when she let herself. But I could tell the sea still made her nervous. Could I really teach her to trust it? And was that the way I wanted to spend my summer? Avery might think we were friends, but I wasn't so sure. Yesterday had been fun, sort of, but the two of us were just so different.

Still, she was here again now, and maybe that was okay. She was nothing like Iggy and Carmen, but she seemed nice enough in her own way. Besides, maybe if I spent enough time with this new girl, Josie and the rest of my family would stop acting as if my sketchpad was my only friend.

We got started right away, paddling out and then sitting there while I explained again how to look for a good wave. Avery nodded in all the right spots, but I caught her gaze darting out toward the pass into the ocean every few seconds.

"Are you listening?" I interrupted myself at last, a little exasperated by how distracted she seemed.

She looked at me sheepishly. "Sorry," she said. "I was just watching for the dolphins."

"They'll be here when they get here," I said. "But if you ever want to be comfortable enough in the water to possibly swim with them, like in your dreams, you'd better pay attention to me, okay?"

She looked surprised. But then she nodded and smiled. "Okay," she said. "Tell me one more time?"

❖ ❖ ❖

We were getting ready to leave the cove on Sunday afternoon, our fourth day surfing together, when I remembered something. "I can't come until afternoon tomorrow," I told Avery. "I have to babysit."

"You babysit?" She looked impressed, as if I'd just told her I was meeting with the Pope or something. "I'm not allowed yet."

"I just started. Actually, I'm starting tomorrow. It's just three days a week, right in my neighborhood." I tried not to sound as apprehensive as I felt. When I'd met with Mrs. Vargas last week, she'd been so outrageously grateful that I was interested—or so she thought, thanks to Josie—that I hadn't had the heart to say no when she'd offered me the job. Besides, I'd realized I really could use the money. That art program wasn't free, and my parents were more likely to say yes if I could offer to help with the fees. Plus, the twins were still young enough to take a nap every day, which would give me some time for sketching—something I hadn't had as much time for as usual because of Avery's lessons. Although somehow, I didn't mind that as much as I'd thought I would. Teaching her was kind of fun.

Avery hoisted her board under her arm and started up the trail. "What time are you finished? Want to meet afterward?"

"Sure. I should be able to leave around four." I couldn't help being flattered that she seemed so worried about missing even one day here at the cove. Then again, it wasn't a complete surprise. She was making a lot of progress. She could bodyboard pretty well now, and while her pop-up still needed work, she'd managed to wobble halfway in on a couple of easy waves the day before. I'd also started making her swim laps with me across the cove so she could get comfortable being out in the deeper water. I think she actually liked that part, especially when the dolphins were around. They always moved away when we came close, but I suppose it was still closer than she'd ever come to living out that dream of hers.

* * *

Tuesday was sunny and hot and still, with nothing but mushy little ankle-buster waves that offered little more than a gentle shove toward shore. We tried surfing anyway, but soon gave up and just floated out in the still center of the cove on our boards, trailing our hands and feet in the cool water. The thick, humid air made me feel lazy and slow; even talking seemed like a lot of effort.

"I wonder where the dolphins are today," Avery said after a while, breaking the silence.

"Don't know." I rolled my head to one side, squinting out toward the passageway into the ocean. "Maybe they'll be here later."

"Maybe."

We lapsed into silence again. I stared up at the cloudless, washed-blue sky. It had been over a week now since I'd sent off my application for the art program, and I hadn't heard a thing since.

Along with the worries that my sketch wasn't good enough, new ones kept popping up. What if the package got lost in the mail? What if I'd mistyped my address on the document? What if, what if . . . ?

I let out a yelp as cold water splashed over my face. "Hey," I said, sitting up on my board so quickly I almost capsized.

Avery was already sitting up, her eyebrows raised to turn her entire face into a question. "Did you hear a word I just said?" she demanded.

"Um . . ." I shrugged. "Sorry. I'm a little distracted today."

"Why?" She trailed her hand in the water, swirling it around to create tiny currents and miniature whirlpools.

My lips started automatically forming the lie:

No reason . . . Didn't sleep well . . . Fight with sister . . .

But I stopped myself. Why not tell her? She'd told me about her fear of the ocean, and about her dolphin dreams, too. She'd even told me a couple of days ago that the real reason she'd moved out here was because her parents were getting divorced. And what had I shared about myself? Not much, really. Avery thought we were friends, but we weren't real ones, not yet. Could we be? I was still skeptical, but there was no way to know for sure if I never bothered to try. Besides, it would be nice to talk to someone about the program. Especially someone who didn't know my family and thus could never give away my secret to anyone who mattered.

I heaved a deep breath of the soupy air. "It's because of, um, this art program I applied for . . ."

I told her the rest, and she listened carefully, seeming interested. "That's so cool!" she said when I'd finished. "I'm sure you'll get in."

That made me smile despite my worries.

"You are? Why? You've never even seen any of my drawings."

That was true. I'd kept my sketchpad hidden from her, making sure it was pushed down deep in my bag whenever Avery was at the cove.

She shrugged, kicking her toes up out of the water and wiggling them. "I can just tell you're talented."

That didn't make any sense at all. But it still made me feel a tiny bit better.

Just then I spotted a dorsal fin coming our way. The dolphins were here!

That woke us up a little, and even made me stop worrying about the art program. After all, what could I do about it?

Seurat and the others didn't seem daunted by the heat at all. They put on a show for us, leaping and flipping and playing tag with one another. We were laughing at their antics when Avery suddenly pointed across the cove.

"Is that another dolphin?" she asked.

I followed her gaze and saw a dorsal fin—smaller and straighter than those of our dolphin friends. "No," I told her. "It's a shark."

As I'd expected she might, she let out a gasp. "A shark?" she exclaimed, already paddling wildly with her feet, trying to turn toward shore.

I leaned over and grabbed the end of her board, stopping it—at least mostly—from going anywhere. "Relax," I said with a laugh. "It's too small to hurt us. Probably just a mud shark, there are lots around here and they don't hurt anything. See? The dolphins aren't paying any attention to it."

That was true, at least mostly. Seurat was the only dolphin who seemed to notice the little shark swimming around nearby. He floated there staring at it, then let out a funny little chirp and dived underwater. I watched for him to surface but saw no sign of him after that.

Avery was watching, too. "Where'd Seurat go?" she said. "Do you think he's scared of the shark?"

"Doubtful." I slid off my board into the water, hanging on and letting my legs dangle down into the cooler depths beneath the sun-warmed surface. "Maybe he just got tired of the heat."

❖ ❖ ❖

The Vargas twins were exhausting. Wednesday was only my second day with them, and I never stopped moving from the moment I arrived—fixing their breakfast, wiping their breakfast off the floor, chasing them down to wipe their hands before they left sticky grape jelly prints on all the furniture, grabbing sharp-edged toys out of the air when they hurled them at each other, racing to block them from letting themselves out of the house, and on and on. Even their naps didn't seem to last more than about ten minutes, which barely gave me enough time to use the bathroom and catch my breath, never mind doing any sketching.

By the time their mother arrived home from work a little before four, I was ready to collapse. But there was no time for that, not today. I stopped at home just long enough to change into my swimsuit and grab my board and then rushed to the cove.

Avery was there, perched on her board at the edge of the water. She jumped to her feet when she heard me coming.

"Ready to surf?" she asked cheerfully. "The waves look pretty nice today, huh?"

"Sure." I barely spared the surf a glance. "But listen, guess what?" I grinned at her. "I've been dying to tell you all day—I had your dream last night!"

"Huh?" She looked confused for a second. But then she widened her eyes. "Wait—you mean you dreamed about swimming with dolphins?"

"Yes." I dropped my board next to hers, still smiling. "It was just like the dreams you told me about, I think. It was incredible!"

"Oh, Maria, that's so awesome!" She grabbed me and pulled me to her, giggling in my ear.

I hugged her back, feeling a little awkward. Avery obviously thought we were friends, but did she really think we were the hugging kind of friends already? Or was she just like Josie, who hugged everyone, even people she'd just met?

"Look!" Avery pulled away and pointed. "The dolphins are here—I was just watching them. Come on, let's go make our dreams come true!"

She laughed and grabbed her board, running into the surf without hesitation. I felt a moment of pride. She'd already come a long way since our first couple of lessons, when she was too scared to push through even the tiniest bit of whitewater without shrieks and drama.

Still, she wasn't quite there yet, either. I couldn't help noticing that she never really dived down deep underwater, preferring to swim within arm's reach of her board, and mostly sticking to a doggy paddle that didn't require putting her head underwater.

But that was okay. She would get there. *Poco a poco*, as my *abuelita* would say.

By the time I caught up, Avery was sitting astride her board, floating in the middle of the cove. The dolphins were half a dozen yards away, chasing and playing around as usual.

"Look, Seurat is here," Avery said. As the spotted dolphin rolled over, she leaned forward, peering at him.

Was she trying to get a better look at his abdomen? I flashed back to what she'd said about that lump, and the dog she knew back home.

But she didn't say anything about any of that, and neither did I.

◆ ◆ ◆

Thursday was breezy and overcast, and the sea looked grumpy with the promise of heavy weather in the near future. Avery noticed, too.

"The waves are kind of big today," she said, clutching her board as we stood on the beach. "Maybe we should just bodyboard."

"No way." I headed into the backwash. "It's easier to surf a stronger wave. Besides, you were so close to getting it yesterday."

That was true. After watching the dolphins for a while, we'd had another surfing lesson. Avery was getting much better at popping up, even if she still looked a little wobbly afterward. A couple of times, she'd managed to stay upright long enough to get more than halfway to the beach before toppling off into the whitewater. She barely panicked at all when that happened anymore, which was good. But it would be even better if she could stay on.

Avery still looked worried, but she didn't argue with me. I was glad. Teaching her was turning out to be more fun than I'd expected, but it had meant me doing a lot less real surfing myself lately. And I was definitely in the mood to catch some good waves today. Maybe it would even take my mind off the fact that I still hadn't heard back from the art program.

We paddled out past the swells, then turned to study the waves. The dolphins weren't around, which was good and bad. It was good because they weren't distracting Avery from surfing. And it was bad because they weren't distracting her from her fears. She looked terrified as I pushed her toward a promising wave.

"Here goes nothing!" she called as she paddled after it.

"That's the spirit!" I yelled with a laugh.

That made her laugh, too. She glanced back over her shoulder at me, and then popped up—and immediately wiped out.

Soon she was back out with me, wet hair in her eyes and a dejected expression on her face. "Told you so," she said. "It's too rough for a grommet like me."

"You're no grommet anymore," I assured her. "Give it another try."

She wiped out twice more after that. I was starting to feel a little discouraged myself. Was I pushing her too hard?

Then she spotted a wave she liked. "Mine!" she cried as she paddled wildly in that direction.

I held my breath as she caught up just before the break. She popped up in one smooth movement, landing steadily on her feet. Sticking her arms out, she bent her knees and rode into it just like I'd taught her.

She rode that thing all the way to the shore, stepping off as neatly as you please onto the wet, rocky sand. The board bumped against her ankle, then retreated to the end of the leash with the receding water, making her stagger a little. But when she turned to face me, a Cheshire-cat grin stretched across her entire face, lighting up the cove more brightly than the cloud-draped sun overhead.

"I did it!" she yelled, pumping her fist. "Did you see that, Maria? I did it!"

I was in a good mood when I headed home that afternoon. The postal truck was just pulling away when I turned the corner, so I grabbed a thick pile of mail out of the box on my way past, flipping idly through in search of the surfing catalog I got sometimes—the only mail that was ever addressed to me, other than the occasional card from Iggy and Carmen or my cousins in Hermosillo.

Except today, there was something else. A slender, crisp white envelope with my name written above the address. My heart thudded; I knew at once what it had to be.

I raced into the house, thankfully empty. After dropping the rest of the mail on the counter, I stared at the envelope in my hand. Then, taking a deep breath, I carefully slit it open with my thumbnail and peeked inside.

13

Avery

A warm gust of wind hit me in the face when I opened the front door the next afternoon. Aunt Janice was right behind me. She'd just arrived home from work, and was already leaving again to meet my mom and Kady at yet another house showing. They'd been looking at properties all week. My mom had told me all about several of them, though I hadn't paid much attention to the details.

"Careful out there today, Aves," my aunt said, sweeping her gaze down over my swimsuit.

"There's a storm coming, and Cam said the water was a little rough this morning."

"I'll be careful." I smiled, thinking back to that perfect wave yesterday. Finally I understood why people loved surfing so much. That had been amazing!

When I got to the cove, Maria was waiting for me. Normally she was kind of still and quiet and patient even when I was late or whatever. But today she was practically hopping up and down with impatience.

"I thought you'd never get here!" she blurted out. "Guess what? I got in!"

It only took a second for my brain to click into gear and realize what she meant. "Seriously?" I exclaimed, dropping my board and grabbing her in a big hug. "Congratulations! That's amazing!"

"Thanks." She was breathless and laughing as she pulled away. "I couldn't believe it when I got the letter yesterday!"

"So what did your family say?" I asked.

Maria shrugged, her smile fading a little. "I haven't told them yet," she said. "My dad and my brother got in a big argument yesterday, so I figured I should wait for a better moment."

"Makes sense." I was happy for her, although it seemed a little odd that she hadn't shared the news with her family, argument or not. "So are you going to show me some of your artwork, or what?"

"Maybe." She hesitated, shooting me a sidelong look. "Do you really want to see it?"

"Of course!" I exclaimed. "I'm dying to see it—especially the ones of the dolphins. Do you have your sketches with you today?"

I glanced toward her bag, which was lying on the beach nearby. Maria stepped toward it, still looking uncertain.

But finally she bent and pulled out a well-worn sketchbook with a purple cover. She clutched it to her chest and took a step toward me.

"I hope you . . ." she began, then stopped and shoved the book into my hands. "Go ahead and look if you want," she mumbled, then turned away to stare out at the water.

I flipped open the sketchbook eagerly, gasping at the drawing on the first page. It was a super detailed picture of a cat watching a bird. The animals looked so alive that I could almost see the cat's tail twitching. "This is amazing!" I cried. "See? I knew you were talented!"

She glanced at me over her shoulder, looking as if she couldn't decide whether to smile or frown. "You mean it?"

"Of course I do!" I flipped from one page to the next, drinking in each piece of art. There were pictures of animals, people, landscapes, and more.

But my favorites were the dolphins. There was a scene of a small pod leaping in front of a sailboat. Another of a slender gray bottlenose gliding along underwater. And several of the familiar pod from the cove.

"Where's the one of Seurat, though?" I asked. "The one you used for your submission, I mean. I don't see a sketch of only him without the rest of the pod."

"It's folded in the back." She reached down and plucked out a piece of white typing paper. "I had to send in the original, so this is just a copy."

I unfolded the paper and gasped again. "Oh, Maria," I said. "I'm not surprised this got you into that art program. It's gorgeous!"

She smiled, then ducked her head so her hair fell over her face. "Okay, that's enough art for now," she said, grabbing the sketchbook and shoving it back into her bag. Then she picked up her board. "Come on, let's surf!"

Aunt Janice had been right. The water was wilder than usual, even in the protected little cove. I tried not to let Maria see that I was scared, though I was pretty sure she could tell. At least, I guessed that was why she only made me try two or three runs before she suggested resting out in the stiller water and watching the dolphins. They'd been there already when we'd arrived, though they weren't very active today, mostly just floating around near the surface and coming up now and then for air.

Even the middle of the cove was rougher than usual. I stayed on my stomach on my board, holding on so I didn't roll off in an especially big swell.

"Look, there's Seurat," I said, spotting the black-and-white dolphin floating near the others. "Let's try to get a little closer."

I still hadn't totally forgotten about that lump I'd felt on his body. Was it as big as I thought? I'd been too scared to think straight at the time, so I had to wonder. Maybe it was nothing. I knew I'd feel better if I could get a closer look at him.

Maria followed as I aimed my board toward the spotted dolphin, kicking gently with her legs. But Seurat moved away as soon as he saw us coming, putting the other dolphins between us and him.

I couldn't help feeling a tiny bit offended, even though I knew that was silly. Seurat was a wild animal. Maybe he just wasn't in the mood to hang out with a couple of humans today. Or maybe the approaching storm was making him nervous, like my old neighbor's golden retriever, who used to wedge himself under the bed at the first grumble of thunder.

At least I hoped it was something like that, and not that Seurat was sick . . .

I was still thinking about the spotted dolphin at dinner that night, letting everyone else's excited talk about the house hunt wash over and around me without really listening. Picking at my chicken stir-fry, I wondered if I should bring up Seurat's lump again to Maria, just in case. She knew a lot about dolphins; maybe she could figure out if we had anything to worry about. I'd tried to look on the Internet after I first felt it but hadn't really found anything useful.

I snapped out of my thoughts when Cam jumped to his feet and poked me on the shoulder. "I'm going down to surf," he said. "Want to tag along? The waves are sick today with all the wind and stuff."

"Are you sure that's a good idea?" Mom shot me a worried look. "Avery isn't the strongest swimmer."

That showed how much she'd been paying attention to me lately! What did she think I was doing all day this past week, anyway? I'd told her about Maria and our lessons, though I hadn't mentioned that those lessons were taking place in an otherwise deserted cove.

"It's fine, Mom." I stood, too, grabbing my plate to carry it to the dishwasher. "I'll probably just watch, anyway."

But I grabbed my board on the way out. Cam noticed and grinned. "Hey, I thought you decided you didn't like surfing."

I shrugged and grinned at him. Obviously he hadn't heard about my lessons with Maria, but that was okay. It would be fun to surprise him with how much I'd learned already. "Maybe I changed my mind," I told him.

Several of Cam's friends were already surfing when we reached the beach. Mohawk guy jogged over.

"Yo, Avery!" he said, obviously surprised to see me. "You came back."

"I came back," I said lightly. "Now what are we waiting for? Let's surf!"

I ran off toward the water without waiting for an answer. I'd sort of forgotten that the waves were quite a bit bigger here than in the cove, but I tried not to think about that as I belly flopped onto my board and paddled out.

When I got beyond the breaking waves and turned to look back in, I felt nervous again. Being here, out in the real ocean, felt a lot different from being in the gentle, sheltered waters of the cove. What had I gotten myself into?

Still, I didn't have much choice now. I had to get back to shore one way or another. Why not at least give it a try?

I imagined Maria's voice urging me on: *Go ahead, Avery*, she would say. *Look for your wave. Be the dolphin!*

That made me smile. Just then I spotted a good wave cresting up nearby. Doing my best to turn off my brain, I zipped after it.

The run wasn't my best. I wobbled some and got a little crooked, and I ended up half-stepping, half-falling off about a dozen feet from shore.

But my pop-up was great. And I didn't panic when I came off, even when the next wave knocked me over and tried to push me down. Instead, I forced myself to my feet, grabbed the board trying to pull away from my ankle, and jogged the rest of the way in.

Cam, Mohawk, and a few of the others were watching. "Whoo-hoo, Aves!" Mohawk shouted, pumping both fists. "Way to go!"

"Yeah, that was awesome." Cam grinned and lifted his hand for a high five. "Have you been practicing without me?"

"Something like that." I pushed my wet hair off my forehead, a little breathless. Maybe I would tell him about Maria and the cove later, when his friends weren't listening. "So come on, aren't the rest of you going to show me what you've got?"

I flopped on the warm sand and caught my breath as they all whooped, grabbed their boards, and raced toward the water. I didn't go in myself after that, but I still enjoyed watching Cam and the rest do their thing.

It was fun, probably the most fun I'd had in a while that didn't involve Maria or dolphins. Who knew? Maybe this California girl life might not be such a terrible idea after all.

14

Maria

By Saturday, I knew I couldn't put it off any longer. I didn't have to send a response to the college for more than two weeks, but that wasn't the point. My mind was filled with all the incredible details of the art program, which I studied online every chance I got, and I couldn't stand not knowing whether I would be able to go or not. It was time to tell my parents that I'd been accepted.

That wasn't going to be easy, and I dragged myself down the hall to the kitchen feeling as if I were marching to my own execution. But I tried not to think that way, doing my best to channel Avery's endless—and sometimes irritating—optimism. She'd asked me every day whether I'd told my family yet, and I could tell she didn't understand why I kept saying no.

Papa was always relaxed and in a good mood on Saturday mornings, not only because he was through with work for the week, but also because he was looking forward to his regular Saturday racquetball game with his friends. He usually made a big breakfast for all of us and asked about our weeks, since he was too busy to check in much while working up to ten or eleven hours a day at the lab.

Today was no different. Over eggs and coffee, Josie chattered endlessly about her nonstop social life, while Nico grunted out a few words about last night's date with Sofia. Our mother had a lot to say, too—apparently there was some kind of shake-up at the company where she worked, though I was too distracted by my own problems to pay much mind to the nitty-gritty.

Eons and epochs seemed to pass before the egg platter was empty and Josie pushed back from the table. "Want me to stick around and clear?" she asked.

"That's okay," I spoke up quickly. "I'll do it."

She looked surprised. "Thanks, Maria. I'll get dinner for you next time, okay?"

Then she was gone, yelling something over her shoulder about a volleyball tournament at the beach. I glanced at Nico, but he appeared rooted to his chair as he sat there picking his teeth with a fingernail.

Mom noticed, too. "Where are your manners?" She snapped. "Hands out of your mouth."

He rolled his eyes but obeyed. I waited for him to leave, but instead he pulled his cell phone out of his pocket, scrolling through his latest messages.

"What are you up to today, son?" Papa leaned back in his seat and studied Nico over the tops of his glasses.

Nico looked up and shrugged. "Not sure yet,"

he said. "Sof is away visiting her grandparents today."

Uh-oh. I hoped that didn't mean he was going to hang around the house all morning. I preferred not to involve either my brother or my sister in the conversation about the art program. It was going to be hard enough to convince my parents that it was a worthwhile use of their hard-earned money without those two butting in. Nico was always teasing me about my silly chicken scratches, as he called my drawings, and Josie liked to tell me that if I spent less time with my nose in my sketchpad, I might notice there was a whole world out there. Which was ridiculous, in my opinion. What did she think I was sketching, if not the world?

"Does that mean you have nothing to do?" Mom asked Nico with a tilt of her eyebrow. "Because you could always help me clean the garage."

That made him jump to his feet at last. "Sorry, Ma, can't," he said, shoving his phone back into his pocket. "I told the guys we could hit up the arcade out on the highway, and I'm the only one with a car."

I blew out a silent sigh of relief as soon as the door slammed behind him. When I turned back, I saw my father reaching for his car keys.

"Papa, wait," I blurted out. "Where are you going?"

He stepped over and tugged gently on my braid. "Where do you think, *m'ija*?" he said with a laugh. "The racquet club."

"Oh." That meant it had to be later than I'd realized. "Um, can I talk to you and Mom about something first?"

My parents traded a surprised look. "Sure, Maria," Mom said. "Sit down, Carlos. Your friends can wait."

Papa shrugged and obeyed. "Okay, what is it?" he asked me.

All the breath suddenly seemed to have deserted my lungs, and my throat felt as parched as the Sonoran Desert. I grabbed my glass, which still had a smidgen of orange juice in it, and gulped it down.

That didn't help much, but I could already see Papa's attention wandering toward the door, and Mom's toward the dishwasher. It was now or never. And as tempting as "never" seemed at that moment, I forced myself to speak.

"I applied for an art program for teens at the community college," I blurted out. "I had to send a sketch, and they only take like thirty percent of the people who apply, and I didn't think I had a chance especially since I'm so young. But I got in!"

"You were among the thirty percent?" Papa looked a bit impressed. "That's my girl!"

"Thanks." I took a deep breath. "So I have to let them know soon if I can come. It's twice a week after school and then a few hours on Saturday mornings, starting in September . . ." I went on to recite all the details I'd memorized from the website, finishing with the cost.

When I said the number, Mom's eyebrows shot up. "Well, it sounds like a fun little program, but that's too much," she said firmly. "We're proud of you for getting in, but I'm afraid you'll have to say thanks but no thanks."

"But, Mom!" I began, my gaze shifting to my father. But Papa was already nodding his agreement.

"Your mother is right," he said. "Every penny we have is already going to you three kids' college funds. There's none to spare for frivolous things."

"Art isn't frivolous." Breathe in, breathe out—don't cry, Maria! "Besides, I can help pay for it myself. My babysitting money . . ."

"Needs to go into your savings account," Mom finished for me. "In any case, it's not only the money. That's quite a time commitment they're asking, and you'll need that time for your studies."

"We're sorry, *m'ija*," Papa added, somehow managing to sound both sympathetic and completely heartless at the same time. He checked his watch. "Now if you'll excuse me . . ."

As eager as he was to head off to his game, I made it out of the house first. I didn't want to cry in front of them. After ducking into the garage just long enough to grab my board, I headed for the cove.

When I got there, the dolphins were playing in their usual spot. Blinking back my tears, I scanned the pod as they jumped and spun, but there was no sign of Seurat, which somehow made me feel even worse, as if he'd heard his picture had gone to waste after all and was snubbing me intentionally.

At least the stormy weather had passed, and the waves were clean and inviting. I wasn't really in the mood for surfing, though, so I paddled out to the still center and just lay there, trying to let the pleasant warmth of the sun on my skin and the squeaks and chirps of the dolphins nearby seep into my sadness.

I wasn't sure how much time had passed when I heard a shout from the beach. Turning my head, I squinted over and saw Avery jogging into the surf with her own board. I didn't really want to see her—I didn't really want to see anyone, except maybe Seurat. But that wasn't for me to decide.

As soon as she saw my face, her smile faded. "What?" she asked, sounding apprehensive. "Who died?"

"My dreams," I said with a sigh. Then I told her what had happened.

She gasped and frowned at all the right spots. When I finished, she just shook her head.

"I don't even know what to say," she said, trailing one hand in the water as her board drifted slowly with the currents. "That's such a bummer. I can't believe they don't see what an amazing opportunity this is for you!"

I shrugged. "They don't see art as an opportunity for anything. They don't believe art can be a real job with a real paycheck, so to them that means it's not worth doing."

"Are you kidding?" Avery exclaimed. "My mom has a friend who's an artist, and she's loaded! She has a lake house and a swimming pool and everything. I can tell your parents about her if you want!"

I just shrugged again. "It won't do any good,"

I told her. "One Anglo lady in the Midwest isn't going to convince them that it's a good choice for their daughter. Not when I could be a scientist or a lawyer of some other *practical* thing instead."

It came out sounding bitter, even to me. "Okay," Avery said. "Did they at least have something nice to say about your amazing drawing of Seurat?"

"They haven't seen it," I told her shortly.

Her blue eyes went as wide as the sea. "What do you mean?" she exclaimed. "You have to show them! Maybe that'll help them understand how important this is to you."

"They won't understand. They don't want to understand." I kicked my legs to stop my board from bumping against hers.

"But, Maria, what can it hurt to try?"

"That's easy for you to say." I glared at her, willing her with my eyes to drop it. "You don't know my family."

"I don't," she agreed. "But I know you, and I can't stand the thought of you giving up on this so easily!"

I rolled my eyes. "You know me? We only met a couple of weeks ago."

"So?"

"So you don't know anything about me—not really." I frowned at her. "You don't even know that we're different people, and I'm not going to do everything you would do."

"I'm not saying that," she insisted. "I just think that if you—"

But I was finished listening. "I think you'd better mind your own business," I interrupted, my voice loud enough to echo off the high rock walls of the cove.

With a kick of my legs, I shot off toward the beach. A nice little wave was just cresting, and I caught it and popped up, riding it all the way to shore. Then I stomped out of the cove without looking back.

15

Avery

"Maria!" I cried.

But she was already disappearing up the trail, only an occasional flash of her brightly colored surfboard showing among the scrubby bushes and trees.

I glanced around, realizing I was all alone in the water—and pretty far out. Far enough that it would only take one stray wild current to sweep me out through the mouth of the cove into the rough, open seas beyond . . .

With a flash of terror, I thrashed both legs so suddenly that I almost tipped off my board. Grabbing the edges, I tried to take a deep breath, but only succeeded in a few shallow, panting gulps of air.

Then a dolphin surfaced nearby. It chirped, then disappeared. But just seeing it made me snap out of my panic, at least mostly. Still holding tightly to my surfboard, I paddled toward the breaking waves. I didn't bother trying to stand up, not now, not when I was all alone out here. Instead I bodyboarded in, tumbling off with relief on the rocky, sandy shore.

I just lay there for a while, staring up at the sky and waiting for my heart to stop racing and my hands to stop shaking. And all the while thinking about Maria and how she'd abandoned me out there, even though she knew about my fear. How could she do that to me? Maybe this proved that she was right. Maybe we really were too different to be friends.

❖ ❖ ❖

On Sunday night, I had the dolphin dream again. Only this time when I woke up it left me feeling sad instead of happy. For a second I couldn't figure out why.

Then I remembered my fight with Maria. I sighed, sat up, and rolled off the air mattress, wondering why she had to be so stubborn.

But that was a question without an answer, as Uncle Phil would say. So I did my best to forget about her. I hadn't visited the cove at all the day before, instead going surfing with Cam and his friends. I was relieved to discover that I was able to put those panicky moments from Saturday aside and have fun. The only bad part was that I hadn't seen even a single dolphin the whole time.

When I let myself out of the bedroom, Kady was coming out of the bathroom wrapped in a towel. Her face was flushed from one of the long, hot showers she loved to take despite her parents' grumbles about the water bill.

"Hi," she said. "I was just going to wake you up. Want to walk over to Center Street with me today? I heard they got some cool new jewelry at the boutique."

I was so shocked I couldn't answer for a second.

That trip to the mall when I'd first seen Maria had been the last thing Kady and I had done together.

Then I remembered hearing her complaining to Aunt Janice yesterday about how all her friends were away at camp or on vacation with their families. So that explained it—she was finally bored enough to hang out with me.

But did I even want to hang out with her? She'd said some pretty nasty—and completely untrue—things about Maria and her family. And even though Maria was mad at me, I couldn't consider myself her friend if I let Kady trash her any longer.

"You know, Maria's brother isn't in a gang," I said calmly. "And her neighborhood isn't scary. I don't know where you heard those things, but they're just not true. You're my cousin, and I think it'd be cool if we could be friends like we were when we were little. But only if you stop saying that awful stuff."

Kady scowled and opened her mouth. But she shut it again without saying anything. I held my breath as she stared at me for a long moment.

Finally she shrugged. "Okay, maybe you're right," she said. "It's not like Maria's that bad, I guess. And I don't even know her brother. Her sister is kind of obnoxious, though. She acts like she's so great at everything." She frowned again for a second. "But whatever, it's not like I hang around in their neighborhood. Maybe it's not like what I've heard."

"It's not," I said.

"Okay." She took a deep breath. "Cam's always telling me I shouldn't talk about stuff I don't know anything about. I guess I should work on that." She gave me a crooked smile. "If I promise to try to be nicer, will you come to the boutique with me?"

I couldn't believe it. I thought Kady would never speak to me again after what I'd just said to her. "Um, sure," I said, even though I hardly ever wore jewelry. "Sounds fun."

It actually was fun, at least sort of. I wasn't that interested in shopping, but Kady could be kind of funny when she wasn't being mean. After we stopped in at all three of the shops that Kady deemed worthwhile on the town's little main street, she led the way to a beauty parlor near the bank.

"I want to make an appointment for a haircut." She cast a critical eye at my tangled mass of hair. "Maybe you should get one, too. You could use a new summer style."

I didn't know about that, but I let her book me in right after her appointment the next day. And what do you know? My shorter "new summer style" turned out to be pretty cool!

* * *

By Wednesday, I was missing the dolphins like crazy. I still hadn't been back to the cove, instead spending my time at the beach with Cam or watching videos and painting my toenails with Kady.

After lunch, I grabbed the binoculars. "I think I'll go to the overlook and see if I can spot any dolphins," I told Kady. "Want to come?"

She wrinkled her nose. "No thanks."

So I ended up at the overlook by myself. I stayed

for over an hour, scanning the water nonstop, but I didn't see any dolphins at all.

Finally I gave up. I was tempted to go to the cove and see if Seurat and the others were there. But going to the cove meant risking another run-in with Maria, and I wasn't in the mood. So I went home instead.

16

Maria

The Vargas twins were miserable and difficult, but at least they kept me busy. For several hours, three days a week, I didn't have a spare moment to think about the art program. Or about my fight with Avery. Or even about how Seurat hadn't showed up at the cove all week.

Not that I was spending as much time as usual there, either. I was afraid that Avery might be just cheerfully clueless enough to not realize she wasn't welcome there anymore.

So on Monday, I tried to see my babysitting job as a silver lining. But by the time Mrs. Vargas got home on Wednesday, I was so desperate for peace and quiet that I rushed to the cove as soon I'd been released from my monster-sitting duty.

When I stepped out onto the rocky little beach, I was half-expecting to see Avery there waiting for me, impatient to get started on our next surfing lesson, hopping from foot to foot in that goofy way she had.

But there was no sign of her. That was good, right? Still, I couldn't help feeling a twinge of disappointment. It seemed she'd really given up on me, then.

None of the dolphins were around at first, but several showed up after I'd been surfing for a while. I floated out as close to them as I dared, trying to let their simple happiness with life rub off on me. But I couldn't help noticing that Seurat wasn't there—again—which made me uneasy. Had he given up on me, too? Or was there something wrong? The comment Avery had made that day about the lump on his belly floated through my mind.

I closed my eyes, picturing the spotted dolphin the way he looked in my sketch, happy and carefree. But thinking about that just reminded me that I still needed to e-mail the art program and tell them I wasn't coming. I knew I should have done it already—just get it over with. But what was the hurry? At least I could wallow in my own dejection for a few days before making it official.

❖ ❖ ❖

That night I had the dolphin dream again. Avery was in it, too, and as soon as I woke up on Thursday morning I had to admit the truth—I missed her.

It was crazy. The two of us were so different. But somehow, during those sun-splashed days in the cove, coaxing her into the water, helping her face her fears, watching the dolphins alongside her, she'd wormed her way into my life. She might not be anything like Iggy and Carmen, but she was the closest thing to a real friend I'd found since losing them. Even if she did have an annoying tendency to meddle in things that were none of her business.

After breakfast, I rode my bike over to Avery's neighborhood. I'd never been to see her at her house, and she'd never been to mine at all, but I knew where Kady lived. Back in fourth grade, her parents had hosted the cast party for the elementary school play—Kady had been the play's star, of course, and I had helped paint the sets. My parents had forced me to go to the party. It hadn't been so bad, since Iggy was there, too, but I still remembered how Kady had wrinkled her nose with distaste at the *cocadas*, the coconut candies that my mom had worked so hard to make for the party.

I'd only made it a block past Center Street when I spotted Avery and Kady just ahead. They were facing my way but they didn't see me, their matching sun-streaked amber heads tipped close together over what looked like a cell phone, both of them laughing. Avery's hair was shorter than the last time I'd seen her; it looked almost like Kady's now.

I stopped my bike, wheeling it behind a panel truck parked at the curb before the two of them— especially Kady—could look up and see me. I stayed there, quiet as a mouse, as the cousins started walking my way. I could hear them from my hiding spot. Kady was doing most of the talking, telling Avery all about the kids in our class and which ones she would want to be friends with. Needless to say, I wasn't on the list.

It seemed to take forever before they made it safely past me. As soon as they'd disappeared around the corner on Center Street, I bolted for home, taking the long way around so there was no chance I'd run into them.

17

Avery

"I thought it never rained in Southern California," I joked as I sat down to breakfast on Sunday morning, glancing toward the window as a gust rattled the panes.

"It usually doesn't, at least not this time of year." Uncle Phil chuckled as he handed me a glass of orange juice. "Looks like it's going to start any second now, though. You two must've brought the weather with you from the Midwest."

"Maybe we did." Mom sounded cheerful. She was flipping through a local real estate booklet as she sipped her coffee. "Does this mean no surfing today, Cam?"

"No way." Cam gulped down a spoonful of cereal. "This weather has the waves macking like crazy! It's going to be epic out there today. Want to come, Avery?"

Kady looked up from her phone. "She's busy," she informed her brother. "We're going to the mall to try on shoes."

"Actually, can I take a rain check on that, Kady?" I smiled weakly. "Get it—rain check?"

She didn't look impressed. "You don't want to go?"

"Not today." Now that Kady had finally decided she liked me, I'd been having fun with her that week. But most of the fun had been stuff she liked to do, and today I wasn't in the mood for shopping or gossiping or whatever.

That didn't mean I wanted to go surfing with Cam, though. The unsettled weather had rolled in yesterday afternoon, and when I'd gone to the overlook to watch for dolphins, the waves had looked scary big down on the beach. I might be getting better at this ocean stuff, but that didn't mean I wanted to take unnecessary risks.

Aunt Janice was bustling around, occasionally checking on some eggs sizzling on the stove while she unloaded the dishwasher. "Maybe we can set up some viewings today," she said, patting me on the shoulder as she hurried past. "You haven't even seen any of the places we've looked at yet. Don't you want some say in where you'll be living?"

"Sure, I guess." I wasn't really in the mood for house hunting, either. For some reason, nothing I could think of sounded that appealing.

After breakfast, I settled for flipping through magazines in the living room. In the kitchen, I could hear my mother on the phone with the Realtor.

Cam poked his head in. "Sure you don't want to come?" he said.

"I'm sure." I smiled at him. "Have fun."

Kady didn't bother to check in, though I could

hear her chatting on the phone with one of her friends as she left a short while later. The magazines weren't really holding my attention, so I tossed them aside and wandered over to look out the window. The sky was clouded over and angry-looking, and wind was whipping the trees around, though it wasn't actually raining yet. I thought about going to the cove, since Maria probably wouldn't be there on such a gloomy day.

Would the dolphins be there? I missed them. Seeing them at a distance from the overlook wasn't the same as watching them play in the cove just a few feet away. Still, the thought of being in the cove alone wasn't that appealing, either. What if something happened? A little prickle of fear tickled my mind as I thought back to how I'd felt after Maria had stomped off the other day, leaving me stranded out on the water all by myself . . .

Just then the doorbell buzzed, making me jump. "I'll get it," I hollered, heading that way.

When I swung open the door, I was surprised to see Maria standing there, almost as if my thoughts had conjured her. "Hi," she said, clutching her sketchbook to her chest. Behind her, a bike leaned against the gate. "Um, are you still mad?"

"Are you?" I countered. "You're the one who ran off."

She flapped her hand as if shooing away my comment. "Whatever. The thing is, I haven't seen Seurat since that day, and I'm starting to get worried about him."

"Since what day?"

"Avery?" my aunt's voice called from inside. "Who is it?"

"It's for me!" I called back. Then I stepped outside and shut the door behind me. The breeze gusted past, making me shiver in my thin T-shirt. "So, when did you last see him?" I asked Maria.

"Not since the day you—the day we—" She shrugged. "Not since the last time I saw you."

"Oh." I did some quick mental math. "Wait—are you sure? I mean, that's more than a week!"

"I know." The little crease in her forehead deepened. "That's why I came."

Now I was worried, too. I tried to remember the last time I'd seen the black-and-white dolphin from the overlook, but I was drawing a blank. Could it have been that long?

"I hope he's okay," I said, thinking again of that weird lump. "Let's check the cove again. With the storm coming, the dolphins might be in there, right?"

I ducked inside just long enough to tell my mom where I was going and ask to borrow a bike. Aunt Janice told me to take Kady's, since she never used it anymore. It was pink, with a big, white wicker basket on the front with a latching lid.

"Fancy," was Maria's only comment when I wheeled it out of the garage.

I rolled my eyes. "Want to put your sketchbook in here?" I said, seeing that she was trying to wedge it into the waistband of her shorts. I flipped open the basket, which was empty other than some dusty old spiderwebs.

Maria hesitated only slightly before dropping the sketchbook into the basket. I dropped the binoculars in there, too, just in case we needed them.

"Let's go," Maria said, hurrying toward her own bike. "It's going to rain soon."

We rode fast to the cove, leaving our bikes tipped over at the top of the trail. Down on the beach, it was less windy, but the spray was still flying, making me squint as I peered out at the water.

"Do you see anything?" I asked, stepping closer to the surf.

Maria just shook her head. "Should have brought my board," she muttered. "It's too hard to see from the beach. Maybe we should swim out there."

"No," I said quickly, shooting a look at the churning, wind-whipped waves. "We'd see if any dolphins were out there. Maybe we should check from the overlook."

"You couldn't think of that when we were at your house?" she muttered. But then she sighed and gave an elaborate shrug. "Fine. Let's go back."

I gritted my teeth, knowing what she was thinking. That I was a big chicken. But I pushed that thought aside quickly. Seurat might need us; this was no time to start arguing again.

We spent another half hour on the overlook with my binoculars before the wind got bad enough to chase us off the cliffs. Once we saw a few dolphins far out, but even though we took turns with the binoculars, we couldn't see Seurat's distinctive, mottled body among the others.

"Where do you think he could be?" I asked as we wheeled our bikes along the sidewalk.

Maria just shook her head. "I don't know. I guess we'll just have to wait and see if he shows up soon."

We stared at each other for a moment, the worry in her dark eyes a mirror of my own state of mind. What had happened to Seurat?

18

Maria

It was raining by dinnertime, and the house felt
stuffy and overcrowded with all the windows shut.
Especially the overcrowded part—once again, half
the world seemed to have decided to show up for
Sunday dinner. My *abuelita* had brought a friend
from the community center along with Aggie. Tia
Teresa and her family arrived in an extra talkative
mood. My second cousin Gil had turned up from
college in search of a home-cooked meal. One of
my dad's racquetball buddies came and brought a
much younger girlfriend who giggled at everything. My mother had invited two single ladies

from the church. Today two of Josie's friends had tagged along, and, of course, Sofia was there, sitting very close to Nico.

There was barely room for everyone in the dining room. I ended up sitting at the overflow table with four-year-old Oscar and Josie's little gang. The older girls all seemed to consider it my duty to entertain my nephew, which meant I had to sit there listening to him babble about some online video game through most of the meal.

That was okay, though. Oscar didn't really seem to notice or care whether I was actually paying attention, so I allowed my mind to drift back to Seurat. Avery had seemed just as worried about him as I was, which somehow made me feel a little better. But not that much better. Since his first visit to the cove, I couldn't remember a time when I hadn't seen Seurat for more than a couple of days in a row. While it was true that I hadn't been there as often lately, it still seemed odd that neither Avery nor I had caught even a brief glimpse of the spotted dolphin since the day of our fight.

Had he sensed the bad feelings between us and decided to leave for more pleasant climes? Or was it what I'd thought before—was he disappointed in my failure to convince my parents to let me go to art camp?

I shook my head, knowing I was being silly but unable to stop those kinds of thoughts from crawling through my head like ants through a melon.

"What?" Oscar demanded, taking my gesture for a response to whatever he was saying at the time. "I did too get the high score, Maria, don't say I didn't!"

His whiny voice was loud enough to cut through the din at the main table. Tia Teresa glanced over.

"Everything okay over there, sweet pea?" she called to Oscar in a singsong voice.

"Don't worry," my sister told her with a smile. "Oscar's in good hands. Didn't you hear, Maria is a real babysitter now!"

"Thanks to our Josie," Papa added with a proud smile for both of us.

I winced as all eyes turned in my direction.

From that point on I had to fend off questions from everyone about my new babysitting career. It was hard not to notice that nobody so much as mentioned the art program, though. It was as if my parents had completely forgotten that whole conversation. I doubted my mother had even bothered to tell Tia Teresa about it, even though she normally told her absolutely everything.

Unfortunately, it was raining too hard to even consider sneaking off to the cove after dinner. Josie and her friends were heading out to a movie, so at least I had our room to myself. I decided to hide out there and sketch to take my mind off everything.

There was just one problem. My sketchpad wasn't in my bag, or the drawer in my bedside table, or on my desk, either. Where had it gone?

I sat on the edge of my bed, trying to think back over the day and figure out where I might have left it. Was it in the cove? It wouldn't be the first time I'd accidentally forgotten it on the beach.

Glancing at the rain-streaked window, I grimaced. If it was there, it would be soaked by now.

"Oh well," I muttered. "Not much I can do about it until tomorrow."

Instead, I grabbed a library book about dolphins that I'd checked out while I was finishing up my sketch. I flipped through it idly, lingering over the nicer photos. When I reached the end, I found the receipt and realized the book was overdue.

I groaned, leaning over to slip the book into my bag. I'd have to be sure to return it tomorrow, and be grateful that at least now I had my own money from babysitting so I didn't have to ask my parents for help to pay the fine.

At least there was that small silver lining in this mostly terrible day.

* * *

Monday was gloomy and windy, but the rain had ended, at least for the moment. I went down to the cove after breakfast, but there was no sign of my sketchpad there—or of the dolphins, either.

I continued on to the small public library. The librarian, a stern-looking Anglo lady with a long nose, observed me with faint suspicion while I dug bills and coins out of my pockets. I'd just finished paying the fine when I heard someone call my name.

It was Zach O'Malley, a boy from my class at school with an unruly strawberry blond cowlick and a toothy grin. He was one of the few boys who talked to me, since we'd had art class together last year and he'd noticed my drawings. He could barely sketch a recognizable stick figure himself, but he had an incredible talent for sculpture, turning lumps of clay into vividly rendered people and animals.

"Maria!" he said, hurrying over as I stepped away from the library's front desk. "How's it going? Guess what?"

That was typical for Zach. He never seemed to stop talking, not even to wait for an answer to his questions. Sure enough, he continued on without me having to say a word.

"I'm doing those art classes at the college this fall!" he said, beaming.

"Really?" I blurted out. "You got in?"

"Yeah." He flashed his face-splitting grin at me. "I sent a bunch of pictures of my stuff, and they practically begged me to come."

I smiled weakly. "Congratulations."

"So what about you?" He gave me what was probably supposed to be a friendly poke on the arm, though it actually hurt a little. "Did you apply?"

"No," I said quickly. "I won't have time for that. Actually, I'm kind of busy right now. See you around."

"Bye," he called after me as I hurried off to hide in the stacks, too flustered to figure out how to maneuver around him toward the exit.

I lurked back there until he'd left, looking through the dolphin books I'd read fifty times already and feeling like the world's biggest loser.

19

Avery

I didn't remember any of my dreams when I woke up on Monday morning, but I had a strange sense of uneasiness. Maybe it was just the weather, which had stayed stormy for most of the night. But my first thoughts were of Seurat, and I decided to go check the overlook right after breakfast. Cam asked if I wanted to go surfing, but I was too distracted, and besides, the waves were probably too big for me in this kind of weather.

When I got ready to go, at first I couldn't remember where I'd left the binoculars. Then it came to me—they had to still be in Kady's bike basket.

I went out to the garage to get them. When I flipped open the basket, I was surprised to see Maria's sketchbook in there, too.

"Guess she forgot about it," I murmured. I flipped it open. The sketches looked just as good in the dim light of the garage as they had under bright sunshine down at the cove. The girl was seriously talented. Too bad her family couldn't appreciate that.

I was sure she had to be missing the book. When I flipped back to the front, I saw that she'd written her name and address on the inside front cover in small, tidy letters. I decided to return it, and maybe see if Maria wanted to help me look for Seurat again.

It only took a few minutes to reach Maria's neighborhood by bike. Instead of hugging the coast, like I did to get to the cove, I turned inland, deeper into the neighborhood. Maria lived on West

Manzanilla Street, and I slowed down to peer at each sign I passed.

A few people were out and about and most of them stared at me as I passed, as if they knew I didn't belong there. I couldn't help remembering what Kady and Cam had said about this part of town.

But I also remembered what Maria had said. And she was the one who lived here. Why should I feel weird? I was just visiting a friend.

So when I spotted an old man washing his car at the curb, I slowed my bike. "Hi," I called to him, trying to sound friendly. "I'm looking for an address . . ."

The man had a thick accent that was a little hard to understand at first. But he was nice, asking me to repeat Maria's address and then pointing the way.

His directions were good. I stopped my bike in front of a one-story stucco house with cheerful blue shutters and a flowering shrub in the front yard. According to the number on the mailbox, this was where Maria lived.

I grabbed Maria's sketchbook out of the basket. Then I left my bike by the mailbox and knocked on the front door.

"Coming!" a girl's voice hollered from inside, though I was pretty sure it wasn't Maria.

I was right. A moment later a teenage girl opened the door.

"Oh," I exclaimed. "It's you!"

It was the girl I'd seen out jogging—the one who'd pointed me to the cove that very first time. I realized I should have figured out that this was Maria's sister, the super popular athlete she'd mentioned a couple of times. After all, this girl had told me her little sister liked hanging out at the cove, and as far as I knew, Maria and I were the only ones who ever went there.

"You must be Josie," I blurted out as Maria's sister stared at me as if trying to figure out who I was. "I'm Avery—Maria's friend?"

Josie looked surprised. "Maria's friend," she

echoed, as if the words were unfamiliar. "Hi, Avery. Sorry, Maria isn't here right now. Want me to give her a message?"

"No thanks, I'll catch up with her later." I started to turn away, keeping the sketchbook hidden behind my back. It wasn't as if I could leave it with Josie, since Maria had told me plenty of times that she didn't show her art to her family.

Then I hesitated. Wasn't that the whole problem? Maybe this was why they didn't get her. Maybe this was why they'd said no to the art program.

"Actually," I said, turning back before Josie could shut the door. "You could give her this for me." I held out the sketchbook. "She left it in my bike basket, and I know she's probably already missing it."

"Is that her book of scribbles?" Josie took the book. "Yeah, she carries this around with her everywhere. I can't believe she forgot it."

"I know, right?" I reached over and opened the book to one of the drawings. "There's some great stuff in here, isn't there? I can't believe your parents won't let her go to that art program."

"What art program?" Josie asked without much interest.

I gave her a quick rundown. "So she got in, even though it's super competitive," I finished. "Probably because the drawing she submitted is so amazing. It's right here—see?"

I took the book back just long enough to open it to the page where Maria had stuck the copy she'd made of her Seurat sketch. Josie stared at it, then flipped back through the book, studying several of the other drawings.

"Wow," she said at last. "These are really good. My sister did them?"

"Uh-huh." I shrugged. "I don't think she showed your parents, though. Maybe that's why they said no to the program."

"Maybe." Josie gazed at a sketch of several birds perched on a power line. "Maybe if I show them they'll change their minds."

"Maybe." I hid my smile until after I'd said good-bye and turned away. I couldn't wait to see Maria's face when she found out she might still have a chance at that program after all!

* * *

The weather cleared up a little after lunch, though it was still cloudy. I took my surfboard down to the cove, eager to see if Maria's parents had changed their minds. She wasn't there, so I sat down to watch for the dolphins. There was no sign of them, though I stayed entertained by some gulls squabbling over a floating wad of seaweed.

After a while I heard someone coming down the trail. I jumped to my feet and turned around. Seconds later Maria burst into the cove, her face bright red.

"You!" she cried as soon as she saw me. She flung her surfboard onto the sand so hard it bounced. "How dare you?"

"Huh?" I took a step back, a little frightened by the fury in her eyes.

She jabbed a finger in my direction. "You had no right to do that!" she yelled. "I can't believe you gave my sketches to my sister, after I told you a million times I didn't want my family to see them!"

"I'm sorry," I blurted out. "I was trying to help. I thought—"

"You didn't think about *me*." Her voice was as sharp as a knife. "Otherwise you wouldn't have done it."

"No, really." I needed to make her understand. "You've helped me so much, you know, with the surfing and everything? I just wanted to pay you back."

"Well, you didn't." She glared at me. "Stay out of my life, okay? I mean it this time."

"Maria, wait!" I cried.

But it was too late. She was already disappearing up the trail, not even bothering to grab her surfboard on the way.

I collapsed on the beach, hardly knowing what to think. I'd tried to help, but instead I'd made things worse. Now Maria never wanted to talk to me again, and that meant I'd lost the only real friend I'd found in this new place.

Burying my face in my hands, I let the tears come, not even caring that it was starting to sprinkle again.

20

Maria

I was still fuming when I shoved my way through the front door, stomping the rain off my clothes on the mat. Hearing voices from the living room, I glanced that way. Josie and my mom were in there, bent over my sketchpad.

I clenched my fists, mad at Avery all over again—and at myself. Why hadn't I grabbed the sketchpad back from Josie when she'd told me about Avery's visit, instead of tearing right back out of the house like my hair was on fire? For that matter, how could I have forgotten my sketchpad in Avery's bike basket in the first place? Stupid, stupid . . .

But it was too late for that. Those sketches were public property now, or at least that was how my family would see it. I steeled myself for the teasing to begin as my mother looked up at my entrance.

"Maria!" she exclaimed. "I'm glad you're here. Why didn't you ever show us these drawings before? They're beautiful!"

"Tell her what you said, Mom," Josie urged. "Tell her you'll reconsider that art thing she wants to do."

"What?" I blurted out, my anger running flat-out into a solid stone wall of surprise that sent it reeling. "You—you will?"

"Maybe." Mom still sounded cautious. "I'll have to discuss it with your father, of course."

"I'll talk to him, too," Josie assured me with the confidence of someone who always got what she wanted. "I know he'll come around when he sees how talented you are. I mean, these could be in a museum!"

I wasn't sure how she could possibly know that, since as far as I knew she hadn't stepped foot in a museum since my grandfather had talked her into coming along with us once when I was little. But it still made me feel good to hear her say it. There was no time to study that feeling, though. I had to figure out if this was really happening, or if I was hallucinating it all. Could my mother really be saying what it sounded like she was saying? Was there still a chance . . . ?

"I don't know about a museum," I said. Then I turned to my mother. "But if you talk to Papa, tell him I should be able to pay most of the fees myself by fall. I can find other babysitting jobs after the twins' grandmother gets back."

"I'll chip in, too," Josie said. "If Papa doesn't want to pay, I'll pay whatever Maria can't. I have money saved up."

I couldn't even respond to that except to stare at her in amazement. Was this really my sister, the one I'd thought barely knew I was alive? The one who thought my sketching was a waste of time that could be better spent socializing? The one so different from me in every way that we might as well be two different species?

"Thanks," I managed at last.

"Sure." She smiled at me. "I mean, I don't really get the whole art thing, you know? I always figured it was more of a hobby. But I can tell from this" —she touched the sketchpad— "that you take it really seriously. I think that's cool, and I want to help you if I can."

Mom looked kind of impressed by Josie's offer, too. "I doubt that will be necessary," she told her. "But I'll let your father know."

"Okay." I tried not to get my hopes up too much. Mom hadn't said yes; she'd only said maybe.

But coming from my parents, that was a breakthrough. And with Josie on my side, maybe it really would turn into a yes!

Excitement and hope flared up inside me, so strong and sweet I felt a little sick. Mostly because mixed in with it was guilt when I remembered yelling at Avery just now. Maybe that hadn't been exactly fair. I was starting to realize that spending so much time by myself meant I might not be the best judge of what people were really like. It was obvious I'd misjudged my sister. Could I have misjudged Avery, too? Yes, she'd gone against my wishes, doing something she knew I wouldn't approve of. But she'd only been trying to help, in her pushy, clumsy, optimistic way. She'd only been trying to be a good friend . . .

A few minutes later I stepped out the front door, planning to see if Avery was still at the cove. But the rain was coming down more steadily, and I figured she'd probably long since headed home by now. I wished I could call her, but I didn't know her number. So I ducked back inside just long enough to pull on a rain jacket, then started off for her house on my bike, the tires swishing along on the wet pavement. I had no idea what I was going to say to her, but I figured I could work that out when the time came.

21

Avery

I felt a little better after a long cry. Well, other than being soaking wet and a little chilly—the rain was falling harder by then, and the breeze off the ocean had picked up, too, tickling my bare arms and legs into gooseflesh.

Wishing I'd ridden my bike, I grabbed my surfboard and turned toward the trail, preparing myself for a long, wet walk home. But just then something out on the water caught my eye—a funny little flash of motion. Turning, I saw that the dolphins had finally arrived.

But what were they doing? Blinking the rain

out of my eyes, I took a step down the beach, trying to get a better look. There had to be at least half a dozen dolphins out there, maybe more, all of them gathered in one spot, bobbing up and down and occasionally disappearing underwater.

When one ducked away out of sight, I gasped as a familiar black-and-white shape behind it came in to view.

"Seurat!" I blurted out, flooded with relief. He hadn't disappeared after all!

But my relief turned quickly to worry. The other dolphins seemed to be gathered around Seurat in a circle. And he was barely moving . . .

My heart pounding with sudden panic, I gripped the edges of my surfboard tightly, wondering what to do. Was Seurat sick or injured? I wished I had my cell phone to call for help, but I didn't usually bring it to the cove, since there was no reception down here, anyway. I thought about running up the trail to tell someone what was happening, but I was afraid that might take too long. What if Seurat disappeared again while I was gone?

No, there was only one thing to do. I gulped as I looked at the breaking waves, which suddenly seemed twenty feet tall. Closing my eyes, I tried not to imagine those waves pushing me under, holding me down . . .

"No," I said aloud. "I'm over that."

I steeled my nerves as best I could and raced out into the surf. The waves really were bigger and rougher than usual—that wasn't just my imagination. When I tried to jump through one, it smacked against me so hard I let out a yelp of surprise. The next wave was right behind it and caught my surfboard, trying to yank it out of my grip.

I managed to hold on, my grip made more desperate when I realized I'd forgotten to attach the leash to my ankle. I almost turned back then. But I forced myself to be brave—for Seurat's sake. He needed help, and there was no one else here. He needed *me*.

Finally I made it to the outside of the break line. I felt a little calmer once I was on my board paddling out toward the dolphins. The water was choppy, but I tried not to worry about that.

"I'm coming, Seurat!" I called, wiping rain out of my eyes.

I don't know if the spotted dolphin heard me. But the others did. Several moved between me and Seurat, almost blocking him from view.

"Please." I wiggled my feet, steering my board to one side. "I'm just trying to help . . ."

I managed to paddle around the nearest dolphin. This was probably the closest I'd been to any of them since that day Seurat had helped save me. But this time I didn't get a comforting feeling from being so close. I just got the feeling they didn't want me to reach Seurat.

No matter what I did, I couldn't seem to get near enough for a good look at the spotted dolphin. The others kept moving him away from me, keeping themselves between us. Finally I thought I had them trapped against a concave part of the cove wall. If I could just get a little closer . . .

"Oh!" I cried as a big gray dolphin suddenly darted in to block me, so close this time that he bumped into the end of my board.

Before I could react, I felt myself tipping sideways. I scrabbled for the board as I tumbled into the water, but my wet, cold fingers couldn't seem to find a grip, and it splurted out and away from me, bumping into the rock wall before the wind-tossed waves carried it off, far out of reach.

22

Maria

Kady answered the door at Avery's place. "What do you want?" she demanded.

"Is Avery here?" I asked.

"No." She closed the door in my face.

I stared at it, fuming and ready to give up. Maybe Avery would come back to the cove tomorrow despite what I'd said. She was stubborn like that.

But I needed to tell someone my exciting news, and she was the only one I could think of who'd appreciate it. If she decided to forgive me, that was . . .

I knocked again. This time the door swung open almost immediately.

"I said she's not here," Kady snapped.

"Who is it?" another voice called from farther into the house. It sounded like Kady's brother. I knew who he was from surfing on the main beach, though I didn't really know him—but Avery had said he was nice.

"Excuse me!" I called as loudly as I could, ignoring Kady's scowl. "I really need to talk to Avery."

Seconds later Cam appeared behind his sister. I wasn't sure he'd recognize me, since he was a few years ahead of me in school and I hardly ever surfed at the main beach anymore, but he nodded when he saw me. "Oh, it's you," he said. "What's up? Been surfing lately?"

"Sort of," I said. "I'm looking for Avery, actually."

"And I already told you she isn't home." Kady sounded snottier than ever.

But Cam looked surprised as he glanced out at

the rain. "Wait, she's not here, and she's not with you?" he said. "So where is she?"

He sounded worried. Suddenly I realized he was right—it was a little strange that none of us knew where Avery was. It wasn't as if she'd decide to just go for a walk in this downpour. Could she possibly still be at the cove despite the rain?

"She probably rode off somewhere on my bike," Kady put in. "She seems to think it's hers all of a sudden, just because Mom said she could borrow it once." She rolled her eyes. "Not that Mom has any right to give away my stuff . . ."

I ignored her, and so did Cam. He was already slipping on a pair of beat-up Vans. "Let's check for the bike," he said.

I followed him to the garage, while Kady just stood there watching from the doorway. The pink bike Avery sometimes rode was standing there with its wicker basket flopped open and empty.

"Maybe she went out to the overlook," Cam said, shutting the garage door again. "She goes there a lot.

Or maybe she went to look for me at the beach—I invited her to come surfing today, but it was raining too hard, so I didn't stay long. I'll go check."

"Okay." I almost went with him. But I had a sudden, strong feeling that Avery wasn't in either of those places. "I'll check the cove."

"The what?" He glanced at me. "Oh, that place she goes with you? She said something about that. But I doubt she's there—Aves isn't much into swimming alone."

I didn't bother to tell him I knew that as well as anyone. We rushed off in opposite directions.

Despite the rain, which was coming down harder than ever, I made it to the cove in record time. I skidded down the trail, which had never seemed so narrow and steep. I was moving so fast that I almost wiped out a couple of times, but somehow I managed to make it to the bottom in one piece. My eyes swept the beach, hoping I'd see Avery there, but it was empty except for my surfboard, which I'd forgotten earlier.

My gaze shifted to the water, and that was when I saw her.

"Avery!" I cried.

She was pretty far out, over near the high, craggy southern wall of the cove, thrashing around like a fish caught in a net. My heart thumped; I knew she had to be terrified. How had she ended up way out there?

It didn't matter. I had to help her. I grabbed my board and raced into the surf. It wasn't until I was past the break that I noticed the dolphins—lots of them. They were swimming around, seeming agitated.

And right in the middle was Seurat. At first I thought he was helping push Avery toward shore again; they were very close together, her arm reaching for his side.

"It's okay, I'm coming!" I called, paddling faster.

She looked toward me. "Maria?" her voice drifted to me over the churn of the choppy waves.

When I neared them, the spotted dolphin disappeared beneath the water, just as he'd done last time. I reached for Avery, ready to pull her onto my board and drag her back to shore again. But she ducked out of reach.

"No, I'm okay," she cried, her hair dark with moisture and plastered to her forehead, her blue eyes wide with worry. "I was trying to help Seurat. I think he's sick or—or something."

I blinked salty spray out of my eyes, confused. But sure enough, Avery didn't seem to be drowning as I'd assumed, or even panicking the way I'd seen her do so many times. She was treading water steadily, turning herself around to scan the waves for the black-and-white dolphin.

"What do you mean, he's sick?" I asked. "What's wrong?"

She swam over and clung on to the edge of my surfboard, gulping in a few deep breaths of the humid air. "I'm not sure," she said. "He was sort of groaning and thrashing around, and the others were acting funny . . ."

I glanced at the dolphins surrounding us. They *were* acting kind of funny, zipping around and bumping into one another now and then. Could Avery be right? Was something really wrong with Seurat?

23

Avery

I clung to Maria's surfboard, glad for the chance to catch my breath but more worried than ever about Seurat. Where had he gone?

"You must have scared him off," I told Maria.

She scanned the cove. "The other dolphins are still hanging around—he's probably still close." She slid off her surfboard. "I'll dive down and look for him."

"Are you sure?" I said.

But she'd already ducked underwater. I stayed where I was, hanging on to her board and trying not to panic as she stayed under—longer, longer. Wasn't this way too long?

Finally she popped back into view, gulping in a deep breath. "You won't believe this," she said breathlessly, grabbing the edge of the board with one hand. "There's a tiny baby dolphin down there!"

"What?" I exclaimed.

She nodded, flipping her sopping wet braid off her shoulder. "Seurat's there, too. I think the baby's in trouble or something, maybe?"

"But . . ." I began.

Then I stopped, since she'd just dived down again. I wished I was a stronger swimmer so I could go with her, because I was having trouble believing what she'd just told me. A baby dolphin? Where had that come from?

I gasped, suddenly realizing what the answer had to be. When Maria resurfaced, I exclaimed, "Seurat isn't a he—she's a she!"

"Yes." Maria met my gaze. "And she just had a baby!" Then she dived back under the water again.

That explained the lump I'd felt on his—her—

belly that time. It also explained Seurat's erratic behavior, and also the agitation of the other dolphins. My mind spun with this huge news. Seurat was a mother!

Finally Maria surfaced again. This time she had to catch her breath for several long seconds before she could speak. "I think the baby is stuck," she blurted out at last. "He's in this crevice, and there's seaweed or something, and Seurat and the others keep trying to help, but they're too big . . ."

"Oh no!" I cried. "This is all my fault—I forced the dolphins over here by the wall!"

Maria looked confused. "Anyway, I think the big dolphins are scaring the baby and making things worse—he keeps wiggling farther into the crevice." A wave splashed up against her face, and she spit out a mouthful of seawater before continuing. "If he doesn't make it to the surface to breathe soon . . ."

She didn't have to finish. I knew as well as she did that dolphins were mammals, not fish. They had to come up to the surface every so often to breathe air or they'd drown, just like humans.

"We have to help the baby!" I exclaimed.

"I told you, I tried." Maria sounded frantic. "But the baby doesn't want me to touch him, and I'm not strong enough to hold on to him . . ."

I gulped, knowing what I had to do. "I'll come down with you this time," I said, my voice shaking. "We'll figure something out together."

"Are you sure?" She looked surprised.

"Yes. You go first—I'll follow you, since you know where the baby is." When she still hesitated, I added, "Go!"

"Okay." She gulped another lungful of air, then dived down.

I closed my eyes for half a second, hoping I could do this. But I didn't have much choice, did I? It was my fault that Seurat's baby was in trouble.

Without giving myself any time to chicken out, I took as deep a breath as I could, and then let go of the surfboard. I tipped downward and pumped with my arms and legs, pushing myself deeper, deeper, deeper . . .

The water was dim and murky down here, but I caught a glimpse of Maria's bright red shorts up ahead. I swam that way, staying focused on my friend, trying not to panic.

Suddenly a dolphin whooshed past me toward the surface, throwing me off course. My head pounded with fear, and I almost turned back. But then I saw Seurat just below—and Maria, too.

A few more strokes and I caught up. That was when I got my first look at the baby. He was tiny and adorable and perfect—but Maria was right, he was wedged so deeply into a jagged crevice that I was afraid we'd never be able to get him loose.

But Maria was already yanking on something. Coming closer, I saw that it was a twisted cord of seaweed. She glanced at me and waved her hand at something on the other side of the crevice, bubbles pouring out of her nose and mouth.

Looking where she was pointing, I saw another wad of seaweed waving in the current. It appeared to be growing out from the same crevice where the baby was stuck, and I realized what Maria was trying to do. If we both yanked on the seaweed at the same time, maybe we could pull it loose—and maybe even pull the baby dolphin out right along with it!

I grabbed the seaweed and pulled as hard as I could, bracing myself against the cove wall. Sharp rocks or coral cut into my bare feet, but I ignored the pain, yanking even harder. My lungs were burning, and I knew I'd have to go up for air soon . . .

Then it happened. I felt something pop, and then I tumbled backward as the seaweed finally came loose. At the same time, the baby dolphin came flying out of the crevice, snout over tail.

A split second later a large black-and-white shape swooped in, herding the baby up toward the surface for its first breaths of air. I was all out of air myself, and for a moment I almost gave up, so relieved that the baby dolphin was safe that I didn't have energy for anything else—but then I felt a strong hand grab my wrist and pull me upward.

24

Maria

When Avery and I finally made it to the surface, Seurat and her baby were already there. Avery choked and gasped, almost sinking down again, but I hauled her over to my board, which was bumping up against the cove wall nearby.

While we both hung on and caught our breath, we watched Seurat and the tiny newborn dolphin swimming nearby. "Wow," Avery said at last. "I can't believe Seurat just had a baby."

I nodded, pretty amazed by that myself. All this time watching Seurat, and I'd had no idea! I wished I had my sketchpad so I could start recording this incredible moment. But I'd have to count on my memory for that.

"We should probably stay right here and keep quiet until she leaves with him," I said. "New mothers can be protective, right? We don't want her to see us as a threat."

Avery looked alarmed. "Good point."

The other dolphins had calmed down a little by then, though they still had Seurat and her baby surrounded in a protective circle. We watched from a safe distance, neither of us saying a word. But after a few minutes, Seurat pushed her way past the other dolphins, swimming toward us with her baby at her side.

"She's coming this way," Avery whispered, sounding awed.

I knew how she felt. Seurat didn't seem scared or angry at all. In fact, I was pretty sure she was bringing her baby over to say hi!

"Do you think she knows we helped rescue her baby?" I wondered aloud.

Avery shrugged. "Dolphins are supposed to be

like the smartest animals there are, right?" She let go of the board and swam a little closer to the dolphins. "Hi, baby!"

I held my breath, still afraid that Seurat might see her approach as a threat. But the mother dolphin swam forward, and the baby followed. Neither of them seemed to mind Avery being so close, so I swam over to join them. The baby was a little clumsy but playful, occasionally even bumping against us and letting out funny little chirps. Avery giggled as she touched his little dorsal fin and he jumped in surprise.

"You know what's happening, right?" I said after a while, glancing out at the other dolphins, now swimming around us calmly. "We're doing it. We're living your dream!"

Avery turned to face me, treading water, her eyes wide and awed. "You're right!" she exclaimed. "Oh wow, Maria. This is amazing! I'm—*we're*—swimming with the dolphins! For real!"

I couldn't help smiling at her, our dumb fight suddenly not seeming that important anymore. So what if we were different; so what if she didn't always do things exactly like I would?

After what we'd just been through, I had the feeling that Avery wouldn't remember our fight, either. But suddenly it seemed very important to say something about it, anyway. I gulped, feeling nervous about actually bringing it up. But Avery had been so brave just now, facing down her fear of the ocean to do what needed to be done. Surely I could be just as brave?

"I'm sorry," I blurted out before I could change my mind. "About earlier, I mean. I freaked out at you, and you didn't deserve that."

She looked surprised. "What do you mean?" she said, stroking Seurat's side as the dolphin swam by.

"I mean, you probably shouldn't have done what you did. But it turned out okay—Josie showed the sketchpad to my mother, and now my parents might let me go to that art program after all."

"Really?" she cried, her face lighting up. "Oh, Maria, that's awesome!"

"I know." I smiled at her, suddenly feeling a

little choked up. "So, you know, I hope you'll for-give me for yelling at you and everything. Because I really want to be friends again."

"We are friends," she said firmly as she swam toward me. "No matter what."

She grabbed me in a big hug, trapping my arms against my sides and sending us both underwater. A second later I felt something large and solid bump me from below, pushing me back up toward the surface—it was Seurat!

Avery and I came up laughing. "Thanks for the rescue, Seurat!" Avery joked.

The spotted dolphin poked me in the side with her snout, then turned away to check on her baby. I grabbed Avery's hand, squeezing it tightly while using the other arm to keep myself afloat.

"Thanks," I said.

"For what?" Avery was watching the baby dol-phin, smiling as it dived down and popped back up again.

"For everything." I thought about my family, the way they were already looking at me differently, thanks to Avery. And how I might get to go to that art program after all. And the fact that I'd found a new friend, even though I'd almost given up after my old friends had moved away. And that even though my new friend and I were just about as different as we could be, we still worked. Sort of like the way Seurat worked as part of her pod, even though she was a whole different kind of dolphin from the others.

"I'm the one who should be thanking you, though," Avery told me, suddenly serious. "If you hadn't helped me with my swimming and stuff, I never would've had the guts to dive down there just now."

"You're totally welcome." I smiled at her, suddenly very glad that she'd wandered into my—our—cove that day. "That's what friends are for."